MEETING AT MIDNIGHT

When Elizabeth's husband Dugald turned up after over two years' separation, she assumed it was because he wanted a divorce, to clear things up once and for all. But the same will that had forced them to marry was now obliging them to stay together—otherwise they both stood to lose their inheritance. Or had Elizabeth got completely the wrong idea about Dugald and their marriage?

Books you will enjoy
by FLORA KIDD

BRIDE FOR A CAPTAIN

For the sake of his young son Tim, Iseult had agreed to marry Nicholas Veryan, a man she hardly knew. And it was for the sake of the boy, Nicholas insisted, that the marriage must be a real one. But surely Nicholas couldn't expect that of her, when he was so clearly still involved with Joanna?

PASSIONATE STRANGER

When Sara accepted an invitation to a concert in California she could not have foreseen that as a result she would be swept back two years—to England, to another life, to the time when she was married to Janos Vaszary. Janos, the man who had taken her heart and broken it in two. Was she ever going to be able to forget him?

PERSONAL AFFAIR

Because she felt sorry for her employer, Greg Lindley, whose marriage had ended so unhappily, Margret was anxious for him to marry Laura Spencer whom he loved and who was so suitable. But it didn't seem likely that Laura would look at Greg as long as his cousin Carl was around. Would it make the situation better or worse if Margret tried to encourage Carl herself?

BEYOND CONTROL

Expediency had been the only reason for Kate marrying Sean Kierly, and immediately after the wedding he had taken himself off. Now, in Ireland, she had met him again—and the natural, sensible thing to do seemed to be to dissolve the marriage. But Kate had fallen in love with Sean at first sight and was still reluctant to divorce him. Yet what was the point of clinging to a man who obviously didn't love her?

MEETING
AT MIDNIGHT

BY

FLORA KIDD

MILLS & BOON LIMITED
15–16 BROOK'S MEWS
LONDON W1A 1DR

All the characters in this book have no existence outside the imagination of the Author, and have no relation whatsoever to anyone bearing the same name or names. They are not even distantly inspired by any individual known or unknown to the Author, and all the incidents are pure invention.

The text of this publication or any part thereof may not be reproduced or transmitted in any form or by any means, electronic or mechanical, including photocopying, recording, storage in an information retrieval system, or otherwise, without the written permission of the publisher.

This book is sold subject to the condition that it shall not, by way of trade or otherwise, be lent, resold, hired out or otherwise circulated without the prior consent of the publisher in any form of binding or cover other than that in which it is published and without a similar condition including this condition being imposed on the subsequent purchaser.

First published 1981
Australian copyright 1981
Philippine copyright 1982
This edition 1982

© Flora Kidd 1981

ISBN 0 263 73735 7

Set in Monophoto Plantin 11 on 12 pt.

Made and printed in Great Britain by
Richard Clay (The Chaucer Press) Ltd,
Bungay, Suffolk

CHAPTER ONE

DARK green pine trees edging the hillside grave-yard whispered together mournfully as a damp wind riffled through their branches. A beam of pale sunlight shafting out from between grey clouds glinted briefly on the pink granite of the old church tower and was gone. Standing alone beside a newly-made grave a tall slim woman, who was wearing a jaunty cap-like black hat on her thick red-gold hair and a black woollen wrap-around coat, stared down at the wreaths lying on top of the grave. Already the delicate petals of the lilies, tulips and daffodils which had been twisted together to make the wreaths were turning brown and wilting under the onslaught of the salty wind, yet they had been placed there only the day before.

Elizabeth Finley Morin sighed regretfully. She had come to late to see her father's elderly cousin, Hunter Finley, before he had died, but she had come as soon as she had heard that he had suffered a serious stroke and might die. He had died while she had been on her way to Scotland from the north-country town where she worked as a librarian in a university library. When she had arrived she had become immediately involved in the arrangements for the funeral. Now that the funeral was over and the friends, neighbours and

5

business acquaintances of Hunter's who had attended it had all gone away, she had come this wet and windy morning, walking up from Nethercraig, the house where Finleys had lived for generations, to pay her last respects to Hunter by herself.

'When I've gone, Elizabeth, you'll be the last of the clan, the last of the real Finleys,' Hunter had often said to her. 'If your father had lived he would have been my heir. Everything—the house, the land and the money I've made—would have gone to him. But he's died before me, so I'll have to make other arrangements. I don't have a son or a daughter of my own, but I like to think of Dugald, my stepson, as my real son, so when I married his mother I adopted him. And since your mother brought you to me I have thought of you as my daughter. It is my dearest wish that you and Dugald should marry one day. It's a dream I have which I have the power to make come true.'

Elizabeth shivered as the wind blowing directly off the sea penetrated her coat. Thrusting her hands into her coat pockets, she lifted her head—and felt shock tingle along her nerves. On the other side of the grave stood a man. Silhouetted against the grey sky, his clothes dark, his black hair lifting in the wind, he could have been the devil come for his due, she thought wildly, and closed her eyes. Surely he was a figment of her imagination, the result of lingering morbidly in the graveyard, thinking morbid thoughts, and he would be gone when she looked across the grave again.

But he was still there, a tall bulky figure who

was wearing a quilted, down-filled parka. His hands were also in his pockets and his shoulders were hunched as if he were feeling cold too. From under straight black eyebrows he was watching her with grey eyes so clear and pale they looked like pieces of glass.

'Jane told me you had walked up here to see the grave,' he said, and his voice was as she remembered it, deep and cool.

'I thought you wouldn't be able to come,' she whispered, staring at him incredulously with wide green eyes.

'You mean you *hoped* I wouldn't be able to come,' he retorted softly.

'Mr Bothwell said that he had contacted the company in Montreal and he was told you were away. He asked for a message to be sent to you but couldn't be sure it would reach you,' she said.

'It reached me,' he replied. 'I set off right away and after travelling most of yesterday, last night and this morning I arrived at the house fifteen minutes ago.' He looked down at the grave. 'There was no way I could get here in time for the funeral,' he added in a low voice as if he were apologising to the man who had died.

The wind moaned in the trees again. Seagulls and crows soared on currents of air. Elizabeth continued to stare at the man who was still looking down at the grave. Two and a half years had gone by since she had last seen him, and during that time she had struggled to come to terms with being separated from him. She had built a life for herself; a life in which he had played no part. Oh yes, he was right, she thought savagely, she had hoped he wouldn't be able to come. She had been managing quite nicely without him.

He looked up suddenly as if sensing her thoughts were about him, and their glances clashed above the grave of the old man who had brought them together and had arranged their marriage.

'I believe we're both expected at the solicitor's office this afternoon for the reading of the will,' he said. 'What time?'

'At two o'clock.'

He pushed back the cuff of his parka. Gold gleamed against the darkness of his wrist.

'It's now almost twelve-thirty,' he said. 'I suggest we have some lunch, then drive into Duncraig together.'

He had always been a formidable organiser, arrogant too, expecting her to fall in with his plans without argument. Elizabeth was tempted to argue with him now, but to do so would be to show that his presence affected her, and she didn't want to do that. She wanted to appear indifferent to him.

'All right,' she agreed coolly. 'Jane is making lunch for me at the house. I daresay there'll be enough for you too.'

Facing the wind, they walked downhill towards Kilford, but before they reached the small summer resort on the shores of the river estuary, they turned off the road down a narrow lane which was really the driveway to Nethercraig. Built of grey granite, the house was situated on a green knoll and looked out over the shining water of the Firth.

As they entered the wide high hallway Jane Brodie, Hunter's housekeeper, came from the kitchen to greet them.

'Aye, I thought ye'd be back together,' she said. 'I've set the table in the dining room for ye. There's fresh made broth, lamb chops, potatoes and green vegetables.'

'I won't be a minute,' Elizabeth excused herself, and went up the stairs.

In the big bedroom at the front of the house on the right side of the landing she took off her coat and hat and washed her hands in the wash-hand basin. As she tidied her hair she peered forward to examine her face in the mirror, making sure that she looked her best. Her fine skin was lightly made up, her lips were tinted a tawny red colour and her green eyes were accentuated by eyeshadow. The sheer black blouse she was wearing with a pencil-slim black woollen skirt suited her fairness. She thought she looked cool, poised and mature, and she hoped she was going to stay looking that way. Whatever happened she mustn't let Dugald get under her skin and irritate her.

He was standing at one of the long windows of the dining room looking out at the view of green lawn stretching away to the edge of the low cliffs which edged the sea, but he turned when he heard her and moved across to take a seat at the table opposite to her. Jane appeared with the bowls of broth and set them down, chatting amiably as usual.

'Ye'll be feeling a wee bit tired, I've no doubt, Mr Morin, after your long journey,' she said.

'Where did ye say you were when the news reached ye?'

'In the Arctic,' he replied laconically and discouragingly.

'Aye, well now, that's a long way to come, so it is,' said Jane. 'And it'll take ye a while to get adjusted to the change in time, so it will. It's wonderful how fast we can travel these days, but I'm sure it doesn't do any of us any good.'

Dugald made no remark. Elizabeth couldn't think of anything to say, so Jane, finding no encouragement to stay, left the room. Elizabeth shook out her table napkin, laid it on her knee and picked up her spoon. As usual the broth tasted of nothing but boiled barley and she reached for the salt and pepper, passing them both to Dugald without looking at him, knowing that he disliked the broth as much as she did and would have to add a lot of seasoning before he could eat it.

'When were you here last?' he asked.

'I came for Christmas and Hogmanay.'

'How was Hunter then?'

'Not very well. His memory was failing and he couldn't walk very far. When did you see him last?'

'In September. I did a little fishing while I was here. He was in good spirits, but was frail, I thought.' He gave her a quick underbrowed glance. 'Didn't he tell you I'd been here?'

'Yes, he did.'

Stilted questions and answers, all about the man who had died, both of them deliberately avoiding the subject which was uppermost in their minds, their strained and uncertain relationship.

Dugald hadn't bothered to contact her, nor had he tried to see her when he had visited Nethercraig last September, yet it wouldn't have taken him long to drive to Brancaster. Oh, why should she care that he hadn't bothered to make contact? At the time she had probably been busy, involved with her work and unable to meet him even if she had wanted to.

Jane came back into the room carrying a tray on which there were two plates heaped with meat, vegetables and gravy. The housekeeper bustled about them chattering and while Dugald answered Jane's questions about Canada Elizabeth studied him out of the corners of her eyes.

He hadn't changed much. His straight wiry black hair showed no signs of greying, although he was almost thirty-five. Perhaps there were a few more lines across the wide brow and carved beside the wide broad-lipped mouth, but the line of his jaw was still clean-cut and he looked as usual in the peak of physical condition. Dressed casually in dark grey corduroy pants, a black high-necked polo shirt over which he wore a heather-coloured Shetland V-necked sweater, he still gave the impression of possessing a rock-like strength; of an earthiness lurking beneath a veneer of sophistication.

The physical strength, the hint of primitiveness, like the blackness of his hair and the warm olive tint of his skin, were inherited from his French-Canadian father, André Morin, that rollicking lover of life and women who had conquered and married prim, shy Kirsty Macray when he had been on a business trip to Scotland. André had snatched Kirsty from beneath the nose of equally prim and shy Hunter Finley, for whom she had worked as a secretary, and had whisked her away to Canada to live there with him. Years later, after André had been killed in a mining accident in Quebec, Kirsty had returned to Scotland to be Hunter's housekeeper and she had brought her young son Dugald with her. All that Dugald had inherited from his mother that Elizabeth recognised were his clear grey eyes and a certain remoteness of manner, an ability to withdraw from people and events when he disapproved of them.

Jane left the room again. Elizabeth looked away from Dugald quickly and at the plate in front of her. The two chops were overcooked and the cabbage was pale and watery. Poor Hunter, she thought, how he must have missed Kirsty, her good cooking, her ability to organise the household, her loving care and kindness. She had died suddenly five years ago from cancer and Jane Brodie had been hired as housekeeper, and although Jane was goodhearted, she was careless and her meals were always disasters.

'We would have eaten better if we'd gone to the hotel for lunch,' Dugald remarked coldly as he attacked the chops on his plate.

'How long are you going to be here?' Elizabeth asked politely.

'That depends.'

'On what?' she snapped the question at him, irritated by his laconic reply.

'On what happens at the solicitor's office this

afternoon. I'm expected back in Montreal next Wednesday for a board meeting, so I hope we can settle Hunter's affairs during the next few days.'

'Where are you going to stay?' she asked.

'In this house. Where else?' He shot a curious glance at her.

'I thought. . . .' Her glance wavered away from the challenge glinting in his eyes down to her plate again. She couldn't eat any more of the over-cooked, tasteless food even at the risk of hurting Jane's feelings by leaving most of it, so she laid her knife and fork neatly together on the plate to show she had finished and looked across at Dugald again. He was doing exactly what she had done and was pushing aside his plate with an ex-pression of distaste on his face. 'Wouldn't you be more comfortable staying at the hotel, since you don't like the food here?' she suggested with a touch of irony.

He gave her another underbrowed glance and one corner of his mouth twisted wryly.

'I get the impression you don't want me to stay here, and yet I have as much right to live in this house as you do,' he drawled. 'Of course, if you find my presence in the house bothers you, you could move out and put up at the hotel yourself. How long are you thinking of staying?'

'For as long as it takes to find out the terms of Hunter's will,' she replied shortly.

'I thought that might be the way of it.' The twist at the corner of his mouth became more marked. 'I expected to find your mother here with you, making sure you got your share of Hunter's loot. Didn't she come?'

'No. She's in Australia visiting her family and she couldn't possibly come for the funeral. She sent a wreath, though, and her condolences, and asked to be excused from attending the funeral,' Elizabeth replied frigidly.

'Good, I'm glad I don't have to tangle with her during my few days here,' he remarked.

'That isn't a very nice thing to say,' she objected.

'Not nice, but honest. She and I were always suspicious of each other,' Dugald retorted with an unrepentant grin. Folding his arms and leaning them on the table, he considered her closely, his eyes diamond-bright between their black lashes. Under that keen survey Elizabeth found it hard to maintain a cool poise. 'You're looking well, Liza,' he said softly. 'Are you still working at the library in Brancaster University?'

'Yes, I am.'

'And do you find the job fulfilling?' he drawled with deliberate provocation.

'I beg your pardon?' Her head up, her back straight, her eyebrows arched in enquiry, she presented a picture of disdainful puzzlement, looking at him as if he lacked a certain amount of intelligence and understanding.

'I'm only recalling your reason for not wanting to go to Canada with me when I asked you over two years ago,' he replied smoothly. 'You said then you wanted to stay in Brancaster, to make a career for yourself, to fulfil yourself . . . whatever that means. And you said you couldn't possibly do that if you were a full-time wife or a mother.' His eyes glittered frostily and his long upper lip took on a sneering curve. 'I do hope that the time of separation hasn't been wasted and that you've managed to find that fulfilment you craved.'

'Wanting to pursue a career wasn't the only reason why I agreed to a separation from you,' she retorted, reminding herself that he was adept at tormenting and had always known how to set fire to her quick redhead's temper.

'There was another reason?' He raised his eyebrows in mocking surprise.

'There were several reasons,' she replied curtly.

'I didn't know that.' He frowned and his eyes were veiled temporarily as he looked down at the congealing food on his plate. After a moment he flicked another ice-cold glance in her direction. 'Would you mind telling me what they were?'

'I'd found out something about you that I didn't like,' she said stiffly. Maybe she could tell him now that she wasn't hurting; now that she was coolly in command of her emotions.

'Such as?' He was frowning again and seemed to have gone a little pale.

'I'd found out about the woman in Montreal,' Elizabeth said calmly, taking her table napkin from her knee and beginning to fold it.

'Which woman?' Was he truly surprised and puzzled? She gave him a quick glance. He was still frowning, but he didn't seem to be at all wary or on the defensive.

'I think her name was Michèle,' she said quickly, smoothing the napkin into its folds. She didn't *think* at all. She *knew* the woman's name was Michèle. The name had been carved on her memory for the past two and a half years.

'That's not an unusual name for a woman from the province of Quebec,' Dugald commented, sitting back in his chair, amusement flitting across his face. 'Michèle what? Didn't she have a last name?'

'I don't know. She didn't sign her last name to the letter she wrote to you saying she was looking forward to your return to Montreal and that she'd made the flat very comfortable and *chic* and she believed you would like the way she had decorated it and furnished it.'

There was a short silence. From the kitchen came the sound of music being played over the transistor radio which Jane seemed to have on all the time. Elizabeth rolled the table napkin and slid it into the silver napkin ring which was engraved with the Finley crest. She was feeling quite pleased with her cool calm reply to Dugald's questions and hoped that for once he was the one who was disconcerted.

'I hadn't realised your knowledge of French was so good,' he said dryly. 'Nor had I realised that you would stoop to reading a letter of mine without telling me that you had.'

The sharp rebuke stabbed right under her guard, finding a vulnerable spot. Inwardly she flinched because she had always felt guilty for having read the letter, but she wasn't going to let his disapproval and obvious contempt for her action sidetrack her now that she had taken the plunge and confronted him with the truth.

'Are you going to deny that you paid the rent for the apartment she referred to?' she accused him lightly.

'No, I'm not, because I did and still do pay the rent on the apartment she referred to,' he retorted coldly.

'Then you won't deny either that you've been seeing this Michèle in Montreal both before and after we were married?' she said hurriedly, and in spite of her attempts to keep her voice low and steady it rose shrilly and shrewishly.

'So that's it,' Dugald said flatly, and putting back his head he laughed. 'You were suspicious of how I spent my spare time when I wasn't with you and you believed I was having an affair with Michèle.' The amusement faded from his face, leaving it looking hard. His mouth curved in a bitter grimace. 'Then why the hell didn't you say so at the time?' he demanded.

'It wasn't funny,' she flared defensively. 'I . . . I . . . was very hurt.'

'And I guess you were too ashamed to admit you'd read a letter which was addressed only to me,' he jibed. 'My God, I had no idea you could be so deceitful!'

'I wasn't deceitful,' she retorted quickly. 'You did all the deceiving, pretending you wanted to marry me because you were crazy about me . . . or so you said. And all the time you were only doing what Hunter had asked you to do. I found out, you see, at the same time I found out about the woman in Montreal, that our marriage was arranged between Hunter and you.'

He stared across the table at her with hooded eyes, his lips set in a tight line.

'What if it was arranged between Hunter and me?' he replied slowly. 'What was wrong with that? Not many marriages are made in heaven, you know,' he added with a touch of derision. 'I admit it. Hunter did advise me to marry you. He had acted *in loco parentis* to me ever since I came to live in this house and he enjoyed giving me what he considered to be sound fatherly advice.' He paused and sighed, then added sombrely, 'But considering how our marriage fell apart so easily I'm beginning to think that perhaps his advice wasn't good after all. You've never been the loving and attentive wife he assured me you would be. In fact you haven't been a wife at all, and I could count on the fingers of one hand the number of whole weeks we lived together before we separated.'

'Well, that wasn't my fault,' she retorted. 'You kept going away.'

'I know I did, because my job demanded I should go away and for no other reason, no matter what you believed,' he replied wearily, rubbing at his eyes with the fingers of one hand as if he was beginning to feel the effects of his long journey. 'But I'm sure Hunter must have suggested to you many times too that his greatest wish was that you and I should marry and have a family.'

'Yes, he did,' she admitted reluctantly. 'But that isn't why I married you.'

'Then why did you marry me? Because your mother suggested it?' he demanded mockingly. 'Didn't she suggest it might benefit both you and her if you pleased Hunter and married me? Didn't she encourage you to make up to me, follow me wherever I went that summer, make love with me, seduce me so that I would be put in the awkward position of having to marry you?'

'No, she did not!' she snapped at him, her cheeks flaming with poppy-red colour as she remembered how she had followed him about that summer almost three years ago when she had fallen in love with him.

'But she made no attempt to interfere, did she?' he jeered. 'In spite of the fact that she hated my guts because Hunter regarded me as his son she didn't warn you about the dangers of rousing the passions of an experienced man who had had more than one love affair before he met you, did she? Oh, no,' he shook his head from side to side, 'not Sandra Finley. She knew too well how to butter her bread to prevent you from becoming involved with me. She even removed herself from the scene, went on holiday for a few weeks by herself so that she wasn't tempted to interfere.' He paused, his mouth twisting unpleasantly again. 'Hunter paid her to go away,' he added nastily.

'Oh, that does it!' Elizabeth sprang to her feet, her resolve not to let him aggravate her swept away by a flood of boiling anger. 'I might have know you wouldn't stay polite for long! But I don't have to listen to you making unpleasant remarks about my mother.' She heaved a shaky breath in an effort to control her voice. 'And I didn't seduce you,' she hissed.

'That's better,' he said, laughter rumbling in his throat, his eyes glinting with devilry as their glance roved intimately over her slim taut figure outlined in black. 'Now you're behaving more like the spitfire I used to know.' Pushing back his chair, he rose to his feet and walked round to meet her as she moved towards the door. 'I'm glad you can still get angry, Liz. It means there's still some life there, dormant under the deep frost,' he drawled, standing right in front of her and blocking the way.

'It's time we left if we want to be at the solicitor's offices at two o'clock,' she said woodenly, looking past him towards the door, wondering vaguely why Jane hadn't brought the dessert in.

'It will take us about half an hour in the car I rented at the airport,' he replied, not moving. Although she wasn't looking at him she could almost feel his glance. Bright as a laser beam, it seemed to be searing her skin. 'Are you going to come with me?' he asked. 'Or are you going in Hunter's car?'

'There's something wrong with Hunter's car and Morton has taken it into Dumfries this morning to have it looked at,' she replied stonily. 'I was going to go to Duncraig by bus.' She hesitated, then added, 'I'd be most obliged if I could come with you.'

'Most obliged, eh? You sound as if it riles you to have to accept my offer.'

'It does,' she said tautly. 'I hate being beholden to you.'

'But you don't have to feel like that, sweetheart,' he said, his voice softening suggestively. 'I'm more than willing to drive you into Duncraig. In fact I'm willing to do anything for you while I'm here. I'll even undertake to melt that deep frost under which you've become buried since we were last together. Perhaps I should start the thawing process now. It might take a few days for it to melt.'

'What do you mean?' she exclaimed suspiciously, stepping back from him. 'What are you going to do?'

'I'm only going to salute you in the way a man usually salutes his wife on meeting her after being separated from her for a long time,' he replied, stepping after her.

'No! Please behave—Jane might come in.' Elizabeth raised her hands ready to place the palms against his chest to push him away.

'To hell with Jane,' he muttered, and reaching out to her waist jerked her sharply towards him so that her head swung back involuntarily, tilting her face upwards.

'If you kiss me now against my will I'll never forgive you!' she threatened stormily. 'You think you can come back into my life and take over again, do what you like. Dugald, let go of me!'

'No.' His hands slid round to her back and she was pressed against his hard muscular body. For a moment his dark tormenting face was poised above hers. 'You like flinging words about in temper,' he taunted. 'You always did. They sound good, but they mean nothing to me. It's what goes on inside you when I kiss you that I'm more interested in.'

'Nothing goes on inside me, nothing, when you kiss me!' she seethed, willing herself to remain detached and objective, watching his eyes lose their clarity and grow smoky as if a fire had been lit within him.

One of his hands slid up her back under the

thick silky mane of her hair and his fingers pressed gently against the nape of her neck. Longing to gasp as sensations of delight needled through her, Elizabeth swallowed hard, set her mouth in a tight line and closed her eyes. She wouldn't fight because to fight with Dugald would only arouse his desires, as she knew only too well from past experience. Fighting him would arouse her passions too. Passive resistance was the best course of action.

Tantalisingly yet dearly familiar, his hard warm lips pressed against hers, moving with subtle persuasion, searching for a way into the fragrant moistness of her mouth while his hand slid round from the small of her back, up over her waist to curve about her breast.

His touch there was almost her undoing. Desire splintered through her in all directions and she groaned deep down in agony. But her lips didn't part and she didn't raise her arms to put them round his neck. She held on to sanity even though her senses were threatening to betray her.

Suddenly Dugald raised his head, and she opened her eyes. They stared at each other, she warily, he challengingly.

'You're making a mistake by playing hard to get,' he whispered. 'You should know me better. The more challenge there is the more I like to overcome it.'

'I'm not playing hard to get,' she retorted, pushing free of him. 'It may come as a surprise to you, but that deep frost you talked about only comes over me when you're about. You don't turn me on any more. The physical attraction which was all there was ever between us has gone, and there's nothing left.'

For a wildly frightening yet strangely exciting moment she thought he was going to behave violently, because his face darkened as blood rushed to it and his eyes blazed with pale demoniac fire. Then he laughed, flinging back his head and showing his strong white teeth, and the rich deep-throated sound mocked her unmercifully.

'Nothing left, eh?' he jeered. The laughter faded from his face as he stepped towards her once more and for the life of her she couldn't have moved away from him if she had tried. 'Oh, I think in the next few days you'll find there's something left, possibly more than you bargained for. You wouldn't be steeling yourself against me if there wasn't a spark of attraction left just waiting to be blown on so that it will blaze up into a fire of passion, the like of which you've not experienced before. And then you'll be wanting me as much as if not more than I want you.'

'Oh, I hate you!' she cried, afraid of his prediction, knowing he could be right, and turning away from him she rushed past him blindly towards the door, colliding with Jane who was just entering, carrying the tray on which there were two dessert dishes. The tray spun from Jane's hands and crashed to the floor. The two dishes cracked, spilling their contents of apple crisp and lumpy yellow custard on the polished parquet floor.

'Oh, dear, I'm sorry!' Elizabeth mumbled, staring down at the mess, her hands pressed to her hot cheeks.

'Och, dinna fash yeself,' said Jane kindly. 'I'll

soon clear it up. And there's plenty more. I'll go
and get it now.'

'No, don't bother. Don't fetch any more right
now.' Dugald's voice was crisp and authoritative
as he stepped over the mess. 'We haven't time to
eat dessert now. We have to go to Duncraig.' He
took hold of Elizabeth's arm and urged her towards the hall. 'You go and get your coat, sweetheart,' he ordered. 'I want to have a word with
Jane. I'll see you outside in the car.'

CHAPTER TWO

IT was difficult to be unaware of Dugald in the front of the little orange car which he had rented because he took up more than his fair share of room, his shoulder nudging against hers, his hand brushing against her thigh every time he reached down to change gear. The only way she could pretend to ignore his presence was to sit as close to the door on her side as she could and look out at the countryside through which the road wound like a grey ribbon.

The wind was still strong, pushing rolling purple-grey clouds lined with silver and gold across the bluish-green curves of the hills. Shadows of the clouds sailed over dark brown furrows of newly-ploughed fields and freshly green meadows, where brown and white cattle grazed. Grey drystone walls edged the roadway, often overgrown with a tangle of rose briars and brambles. Sometimes the walls gave way to thick copses of dark spruce and ghostlike silver birches, tassled with yellow catkins.

The scene was very familiar to Elizabeth because she had travelled that road many times during the past nine and a half years and in all that time there had been few changes. Perhaps the road had been widened in a few places. Perhaps a new barn had been added to one of the scattered farms. Otherwise the gently rolling land was just the same as it had always been, neat and well-preserved, cared for by a people who valued every grain of soil, every blade of grass and every tree.

She had been fifteen, sad at heart and slightly disorientated, when she had first come to Nethercraig, invited there by Hunter when he had heard of the death of his cousin and only blood relative, Arthur Finley, her father. She had been sad at heart because she had missed her father desperately and she had been disorientated because it had been the first time she had been in Britain. Although British born, Arthur Finley had lived and worked most of his life in Australia. He had married an Australian woman and his daughter had been born and had grown up in an Australian city.

Everything had seemed very small, very green and very neat to her when she had first come along this road with her mother, riding in Hunter's stately car driven by Bob Morton, his chauffeur, who had met them at Dumfries. She had felt like a stranger and had been quite prepared to dislike the relative she had never met before. But she hadn't been allowed to feel like a stranger for long. The warmhearted, family-conscious Hunter had made her feel welcome in his house and so had his wife Kirsty. Both of them had seemed to sense her closeness to her father and Hunter in particular had gone out of his way to fill the gap in her life, taking a fatherly interest in her plans for her future and encouraging her to look for a career to follow.

'We want you to stay here and make this your

home for as long as you want,' he had said to her
and her mother after they had been at Nethercraig
for two weeks. And that was what Sandra had
decided to do. She had soon found a job as a lab-
oratory technician in a nearby town and Elizabeth
had been placed in the High School in the same
town.

Dugald had not been living at Nethercraig then
because after graduating as a geologist from a
Scottish university he had gone back to Canada
to work on geological surveys for a mining company. Hunter had talked about him often, much
more than Kirsty had done, and so much that
Sandra had often become very irritated with the
old man.

'You'd think Dugald was his own son, the
way he talks,' she had remarked once to
Elizabeth.

'Well, he has adopted him,' Elizabeth had
pointed out.

'I expect Kirsty encouraged him to do that.
From all accounts it didn't take her long to make
herself indispensable to Hunter when she took on
the job as housekeeper here and to persuade him
to marry her. She would have her eye on the
money. It must have been quite a blow to her
hopes for herself and her precious son when we
came here and Hunter asked us to stay and live
here.'

'Why would it be a blow to them?' Elizabeth
had asked innocently.

'Because Hunter's very clannish. He likes to put
blood relations first, so he's bound to leave most
of his fortune, if not all of it, to you rather than to

someone who's only a relation through marriage and adoption.'

'Fortune? Is Hunter rich, then?' Elizabeth had been naïvely surprised.

'Of course he is.' Sandra had given her a scathing green-eyed glance. 'Can't you tell by this house? Really, Liza, you're very like your father at times! You never seem to see what's right under your nose. Haven't you noticed the beautiful antiques, and the original paintings? Look at the way the garden is landscaped and kept. Hunter can afford not only a wife but a chauffeur, two gardeners and a woman to clean the house. He's worth over a million pounds.'

'How did he make so much money?' Elizabeth had exclaimed.

'Property development. He started life as an electrician wiring new houses, became interested in buying land at low prices on which he was able to build houses speculatively to sell at inflated prices.'

'He doesn't behave like a rich man, though,' Elizabeth had remarked. She had always imagined wealthy men to be overbearing and aggressive. 'I mean, he's quiet and gentle.'

'He can afford to be,' Sandra had said dryly.

'I like him.'

'I'm glad you do,' Sandra had said in her forthright way. 'And fortunately he likes you. So just you see to it that you don't offend him in any way. Always aim to please him and you'll benefit in the long run and so shall I.'

Innocent of the ways of the world at that time, in love with life, Elizabeth had found her mother's remarks puzzling for a while but had soon forgotten them. Now, looking back in the light of what Dugald had said about her mother, she wondered if he was right and Sandra had encouraged her to do whatever Hunter had advised because she had known that marriage to Dugald would benefit not only her daughter financially but also herself.

After finishing high school she had studied at a polytechnic college to be a librarian, leaving Nethercraig to live in the city where the college had been situated, and she had soon been absorbed by her studies and student activities, falling in and out of love periodically with some of the young men she had met but taking none of the friendships seriously. Her aim had been to qualify as a librarian and to find a job which would make her independent.

She had been almost twenty-one and had just completed her second year of study when she had met Dugald for the first time. Returning as usual to Nethercraig for the summer holidays, she had found him in residence there. He had been on three months' leave from the company for which he had worked then and had decided to spend most of it in Scotland.

Their initial meeting had had a strange quality. Both of them had heard much about the other from Hunter and possibly each of them had been prepared to dislike and resent the other. Even now Elizabeth could remember how warily they had approached each other in the cosy littered sunporch where Hunter had liked to sit in the afternoons. They had shaken hands quickly, both pulling their hands back sharply as if the touch had given each of them a shock, both backing away, although their glances had stayed fixed, his diamond-bright assessing her hair, her face and her figure; hers wide and wondering, observing everything about him.

Physically he had been overpowering—tall, yet wide, with ox-like shoulders and a broad chest across which his grey denim shirt had strained so that the buttons had looked as if they might have popped off at any moment, he had been so dark-haired and sallow-skinned that she had thought Kirsty had named him well when she had had him christened Dugald, the name derived from the Gaelic *Dughall* and meaning *Black Stranger*.

But his free and easy manners had offended her, so had his rough and casual way of speaking. There had been an arrogance about him that had grated on her nerves. Impressed as she had been at that time by the Women's Liberation movement, Dugald had represented for her the epitome of male *machismo*, and she had been determined to ignore him while they were both staying at Nethercraig.

It had been impossible for her to ignore him or avoid him. Not that he had made any effort to seek her out at first. In fact he had seemed to ignore her. But living in the same house they had been unable to avoid meeting every day at some meal or other; or on the stairs or in the hallway or in the garden or on the driveway. And even when they had left the house to go to the village they had run into each other, because they had both had the same interest in sailing and had been members of the small summer sailing club.

Sometimes they had been invited to a party at the same houses and inevitably he had been placed in the position of having to offer her a lift back to Nethercraig in his car, and reluctantly Elizabeth had been placed in the position of having to accept his offer and had ridden home in the darkness beside him, tensely aware as she was now, of his powerful masculinity and its threat to her peace of mind.

For over two weeks they had apparently ignored each other, but in reality had watched each other stealthily, like two sworn enemies before attacking. Dugald had attacked first, accusing her one day of following him about.

'I don't follow you,' she had flashed angrily. 'Can I help it if you're always where I want to be? If you're at the sailing club when I go there or in the village pub when I call in with my friends for a drink in the evening? It's a free country and I can go anywhere I like. Anyway, I wouldn't follow you about if you were the last man on earth and I were the last woman!'

'Wouldn't you?' He had flung back his head and had laughed heartily, his big white teeth flashing against the olive-dark colour of his face, the strong tanned column of his throat arching back, and somewhere in the region of her stomach she had experienced a new sensation, a tautness which had been, she realised now, the first awakening of physical desire. 'If I were the only man and you were the only woman on the earth you'd follow me about, all right. I'd follow you, too. You can be sure of that,' he had retorted.

They had been in the woods behind Nethercraig, on the pathway which led over the hill to the village. She had been on her way to the sailing club to meet a friend to go sailing when Dugald had emerged suddenly from behind the trunk of a tree and had blocked the path. Standing in front of her, his hands set casually on his hips, he had been darkly menacing.

'Why would you follow me if I were the only woman on the earth?' she had challenged, tossing back her head, her bright hair sparkling with fiery lights in the shafts of sunlight which had penetrated the green-gloom of the woods.

'Because I'd want you,' he had replied bluntly but softly, leaning towards her. 'And I would want to do this,' he had added, and before she had been able to move away he had bent his head and had kissed her.

She had fought. She had kicked his shins and had pummelled his arms and shoulders with her fists. She had tried every move she had learned at the college karate classes in an attempt to break free of his bear-like hug. The more she had struggled the tighter he had hugged her and the harder his lips had pressed against hers, until suddenly the desire which had been fluttering and tingling within her had surged upwards. Her body had grown limp and had moulded itself against his. She had clung to him shamelessly, feeling and enjoying for the first time in her life the touch of a man's hands on her skin, the possession of her mouth by his.

Dugald had lifted his head at last and her head had fallen forward to lie like a rag doll's against the broad expanse of his shoulder. Both breathless, they had drawn great gulps of resin-scented air into their lungs and all about them the trees had sighed softly in the breeze and the birds had sung joyously. In Elizabeth's hair his fingers had been surprisingly gentle, smoothing it and eventually tugging it to get her to lift her face from the cotton-sheathed bulge of his shoulder to look up at him.

'You fight like a tigress, lady,' he mocked. 'You've clawed and scratched me.'

'You hug like a bear,' she had retorted. 'You've squeezed and bruised me!'

And then, for no apparent reason, they had started to laugh. Their arms had reached out again in a joyful natural embrace as if both of them had been glad to admit at last that they had been attracted to each other. A violent, magnetic attraction it had been; an attraction of opposites of fair to dark and dark to fair; of daintiness and fastidiousness to tough strength and rough casual manners and vice versa; an attraction against which they had both struggled and which they had both resented.

Neither of them had been aware of the passage of time that morning as they had wandered about hand in hand, talking and often embracing. Elizabeth hadn't gone to meet her friend that day, nor had she gone anywhere without Dugald during the next few weeks. They had become almost inseparable, finding it hard to part at the end of each day and to go to their separate rooms at night, and the culmination of the intense fascination each had had for the other had come one night in a flare-up of sensual passion on the small island of Mindoon.

Mindoon was part of the estate owned by Hunter, and its pink granite rocks topped by green grass and scattered whin bushes could be seen every day from the front windows of the house. It was attached to the mainland by a causeway of mud and shingle, created by the waters which swirled together from different directions around the island. Across the causeway it was possible to walk to the island when the tide was out.

One afternoon when the tide had been out at the convenient hour of three o'clock Hunter had asked Dugald to walk over to the island to check on the cottage there which he often let to holiday-makers. Hunter had wanted to make sure that the tenants who had just vacated the cottage had left it clean and tidy and properly locked up. And of course Dugald had invited Elizabeth to go with him.

After making sure that the cottage was in good condition they had walked to the farthest extent of the island where an automatic lighthouse flashed a message of warning to fishermen and yachtsmen. They had been so absorbed in each other as usual that they had forgotten the time. When they had returned to the other side of the island the causeway had disappeared under grey wind-lashed waves and the wind had been increasing in strength.

'Maybe Hunter will ask one of the fishermen to

come out in his boat to fetch us,' Elizabeth had said.

'And maybe he won't,' Dugald had replied, looking up at the sky. 'Looks like we're in for a gale tonight, and no self-respecting fisherman is going to risk his boat or his neck coming for us when he knows we're perfectly safe here and have shelter. Let's go back to the cottage and see if the last people left any canned food. I'm beginning to feel hungry.'

His calm acceptance of the situation had re-assured her. In fact, looking back now, she realised she had been glad they had been stranded together. Back at the cottage Dugald had lit a fire in the old stone hearth and they had found tinned soup, tea and instant coffee in a cupboard. It had been fun playing house together and after they had eaten they had sat in front of the fire on an old sofa. Quite naturally they had begun to embrace each other as they had talked, slowly going a little further and a little further until both of them had been so aroused that withdrawal would have been painful. Into the main bedroom Dugald had carried her and there on the bed they had made love freely and passionately until they had fallen asleep in each other's arms, awakening at first light, hungry but happy to be together, only to find that they had missed the low tide and the causeway had been covered again by the sea.

But the wind had died down and it hadn't been long before a small fishing boat had appeared, chugging round from Kilford, sent by Hunter to rescue them.

'I'd like to marry you before I go back to Canada,' Dugald had said as they had walked back to Nethercraig from the village where they had been put ashore.

'Because of what happened on the island?' Elizabeth had asked, suddenly suspicious of his motives because he was talking marriage after knowing her only three and a half weeks. 'You don't have to,' she had continued proudly. 'I don't expect you to.'

'No, not because of what happened on the island,' he had replied, swinging her round to face him. He had framed her face with strong but gentle hands and had gazed at her with eyes that had blazed smokily with desire. 'But because I want to, because I'm crazy about you,' he had whispered. 'I want you to be mine always, Liza.'

'But I can't marry you, not yet,' she had muttered. 'I want to finish my training. I have another year's study to do before I take my finals, so I can't get married yet. Couldn't you wait until next year?'

'I don't see why either of us should wait,' he had argued. 'We could marry and you could stay here to finish your training while I go back to Canada. I'll be working in some pretty remote places where I couldn't take you, so you might as well be here, studying. I'll come and visit you whenever I can.' His hands had left her face to grip her arms. 'Say yes, Liza, please say yes,' he had urged her.

And recalling the delights of the night, still swinging on the high which his lovemaking had induced, she had said yes, and they had gone into the house and told Hunter. The old man had been delighted and had insisted that Elizabeth inform her mother at once so that Sandra would return from a holiday which she had unexpectedly decided to take to make the wedding arrangements. Three and a half weeks later Elizabeth and Dugald had taken their vows at the village church and after a brief whirlwind honeymoon on Skye, Dugald had left for Canada and she returned to college.

They had met again at Christmas that year when he had flown over to join her and Nethercraig. Their reunion had been passionate and their time together all too short, so that when he had been ready to leave she had almost given in to her own weaknesses and had gone with him. Strangely he had argued against her going with him.

'Not yet. I'll be going to South America soon to work on a survey there, so there isn't much point in you coming over to Canada just to live there by yourself. Finish your studies, get that qualification you're so keen on, then once I've come back from South America and you're qualified we can get together and make a home in Montreal. That's something we can plan for and look forward to. Don't worry, sweetheart, we'll meet again in the summer.'

Dugald had still been in South America when Elizabeth had qualified at last. Delighted by her own success, she had informed him by cable and he had cabled back his congratulations. Later he had written, very briefly, to say he would not be able to see her in the summer as he had promised but that he hoped to see her at Nethercraig at the end of August possibly for the celebration of their first wedding anniversary.

Naturally she had been disappointed because he had been delayed, but the disappointment had been offset when the professor with whom she had studied had suggested she take a job as an assistant librarian in Brancaster University Library and combine her work with studies for a master's degree.

'I can't give you an answer yet,' she had told him. 'I'll have to discuss it with Dugald.'

'Dugald?' he had queried.

'My husband. He's away just now in South America.'

'Then you don't live together?'

'Not much,' she had admitted.

'Then why did you get married?'

'I . . . I . . . suppose it was because we were in love with each other,' she had replied.

'Were in love? Aren't you in love with him now?'

'I . . . oh, yes, I am,' she had replied hastily. 'Will it be all right if I give you an answer at the end of August or the beginning of September? You see, I'm not expecting Dugald back until then.'

'Yes, that will be all right, but don't leave it any later than the fifteenth of September.'

She had spent a pleasant holiday at Nethercraig with Hunter, meeting old friends, sailing in the estuary and looking forward to Dugald's arrival. But he hadn't come for their anniversary. Instead a cable had arrived from him saying he was delayed on business in Montreal but would be with her at the beginning of September and wishing her many happy returns of their anniversary. The same day a huge sheaf of salmon pink gladioli, the flowers which had decorated the church on their wedding day, had arrived for her, sent by Dugald with all his love.

Although she had been pleased because he had remembered the anniversary her pleasure had been spoilt by the doubts which had begun to niggle in her mind. They had been planted there by her friend Fiona Edgar, whom she had known ever since she had gone to live at Nethercraig. A few years older than Elizabeth, Fiona had known Dugald long before Elizabeth had arrived on the scene. A small woman with dark brown hair and deep Celtic blue eyes, Fiona was a teacher and had often spent her holidays in her parents' summer cottage at Kilford.

'The flowers are lovely,' Fiona had said as she had helped Elizabeth arrange the stiff spikes of gladioli on a big pottery jug in the sitting room at Nethercraig. 'But doesn't such extravagance make you just a little suspicious of Dugald?'

'No. Why should it?' Elizabeth had asked.

'Don't you feel he's trying to divert you ... soft-soap you to prevent you from asking why he's delayed in Montreal?'

'He's told me why he's delayed. On business— I expect he has to attend meetings at the headquarters of his company, which are in Montreal.'

'On business,' repeated Fiona wryly. 'And what

a multitude of sins that's covered for a man in the past, and in the present, too! Are you sure it's the only reason he's delayed? Hasn't it ever occurred to you that he might be spending time there with another woman? He does have a woman friend there, you know.'

'Does he?' Elizabeth had retorted, pretending to be indifferent. 'How do you know he has?'

'He's told me about her.' Fiona had smiled a slight secretive smile as she pushed another spike of flowers into the jug. 'Dugald used to tell me everything about himself. We were very close friends before. ... .' She had broken off and had sighed. 'I was very upset when he told me he was going to marry you. I didn't see how he could do it.'

'Do what?' Elizabeth had questioned flatly, and Fiona's vivid blue eyes had regarded her coldly.

'Marry you when he was in love with another woman,' she had replied, then had added bitterly, 'But then men have always been capable of doing that, especially when it's been pointed out to them that a marriage could be financially beneficial. When I told him my concern he said he was marrying you to please Mr Finley. He said the marriage was arranged so that you and he could inherit Mr Finley's property when he dies. Did you know about the arrangement?'

'Of course I did,' Elizabeth had replied coolly. 'Hunter talked of nothing else from the time I first came to this house.' She had managed to look directly at Fiona and had laughed. 'Don't look so surprised, Fiona. Why do you think I agreed to marry Dugald? It wasn't for purely romantic reasons, you know. I'd known for a long time that I would benefit in the long run if I married him. I married to please Hunter, too.'

She had been quite pleased with the show of cool unconcern she had been able to put on before Fiona, but later, in the privacy of her bedroom, she had been racked with mixed emotions, jealousy of the unknown and until that day unheard-of woman in Montreal being uppermost. Tortured by the thought that while she waited for him to come and join her at Nethercraig Dugald was dallying in Montreal with a woman, she had come to a decision. She would wait for him no longer.

Hunter had been upset the next day when she had told him she was leaving and returning to Brancaster to work in the university library, but she had not allowed his sentiments to stop her from going.

'Dugald will understand,' she had told him. 'He likes to lead his own life, so he won't object to me leading mine, even if we are married.'

By the end of the week she had taken up the position at the library and had also committed herself to studying for a master's degree in librarianship. One day when she had been leaving the library at the end of the day's work she had found Dugald waiting for her in the entrance hall. Both of them had been too overwhelmed by the pleasure of being together to spoil their first hours alone by asking questions. The loving had come first, the questions much later, next morning in fact, when they had been drowsily embracing in the snugness of the bed at the flat which she had rented.

'Do you love me?' Elizabeth had asked.

'I wouldn't be here if I didn't,' Dugald had replied, and had prevented further questions by kissing her, and once again passion had flared between them. Much later he had asked, 'Are you coming to Canada with me when I go back there the day after to-morrow?'

'So soon?' she had exclaimed, shifting away from him a little so that she could see his face. 'I thought you would have a month's leave at least, you've been away for so long.'

'I did have a month's leave, but I used most of it up before I came to Scotland,' he had replied.

'Where?' she had demanded, feeling jealousy spring up.

'In Montreal.'

'Why?'

'I had some important business to attend to,' he had evaded.

'What sort of business?'

'You'll find out when you get there,' he had replied, the slight smile which had always seemed to mock her curving his mouth as he had moved away from her to lie on his back, but his evasions had only served to increase her suspicious doubts about him.

'I'm not going with you,' she had said.

'Why not?' He had turned his head to look at her, his eyes narrow and sharp.

'I have a job at the university library and

Professor Williams has suggested I take another degree while I'm working at the library.'

'How long will that take?' he had asked. He had been very still, she remembered, and his voice had been very quiet.

'About two years.'

Dugald hadn't said anything. His eyes had closed, heavy black-fringed eyelids covering their bright clarity, and after a while she had begun to think he had fallen asleep.

'Dugald,' she had whispered, shifting closer to him, sliding a bare leg intimately across his, laying one hand palm downwards on the rough hair of his chest. He had opened his eyes then and had looked at her.

'I guess it means a lot to you, having the job and studying for that extra degree,' he had said.

'Yes, it does. It means as much to me as your work means to you.'

'And more than I mean to you,' he had accused, his mouth twisting sardonically.

'I didn't say that,' she had objected.

'You didn't have to. It's obvious,' he had drawled. 'You wouldn't have come here and taken the job if I'd meant more to you than it does. You'd have waited at Nethercraig for me as we'd planned.' He had sat up suddenly and had pushed the bedclothes aside. 'Okay, stay here and do your thing. You don't have to come with me,' he had said coldly as he had slid off the bed and had gone over to the chair where he had laid his clothes. 'But don't expect me to come and see you all the time. I'm going to be pretty busy myself during the next couple of years. With a couple of other guys I know I'm starting a mining development company.' In the process of pulling on his trousers he had given her a sharp speculative glance. 'Maybe we should separate,' he had drawled.

'Separate?' Elizabeth had exclaimed, lunging up in the bed, hugging the sheet about her. 'What do you mean?'

'I mean we won't live together.' He had grinned rather wryly. 'It won't be much different from the way we've lived for the past twelve months except that neither of us will be under an obligation to visit each other regularly. It should suit us both very well considering the circumstances, my work being in Canada and yours being here.' He had finished fastening his belt buckle and had looked at her again. 'We'll still be legally married but we won't expect too much of each other. Do you agree?'

'I don't know,' she had cried wildly, and had experienced a deep ravaging ache of disappointment because he hadn't bothered to even attempt to persuade her to go with him to Canada. 'I'll have to think about it.'

'Well, don't take too long about your thinking, because I'll be leaving after breakfast to go back to Nethercraig. I promised I would call in again to see Hunter before returning to Montreal tomorrow.' From the bedroom doorway he had given her another challenging glance and had added quietly, 'It's up to you, Elizabeth. You can come with me to Montreal and make a home for both of us there, or you can stay here and we'll separate for a while.'

His coldness, even the way he had used her full given name instead of the usual affectionate Liza or Liz had seemed to emphasise for her how much he had separated himself from her already.

'Then you lied to me just now when you said you were here because you love me,' she had accused stormily, shaken by hurt and bewilderment. 'If you loved me you wouldn't talk about separation. You don't love me and you have never loved me. You didn't marry me for love.'

'Can you honestly say you married me for love?' he had retorted, his eyes beginning to glitter as his own temper rose. 'If you'd married me for love you'd give up this idea of working here and taking a further degree and come with me to Canada as we planned when we were married last year.' He had raked a hand through his tousled black hair and had taken a few paces about the room, impatience showing in every move he had made. 'I realise my views on marriage may seem a little old-fashioned to you,' he had said, his voice rasping angrily as he had swung round to glare at her, 'but I would like my wife to make a home for me to come back to when I've finished working. I'd like her to have my children and to look after them.'

'Then you'll have to get yourself another wife. I'm not ready to be a full-time wife or to have children,' she had retorted. 'I want to find out if I can hold a job down and support myself. I want to fulfil my potential and I'd thought that you . . .' her voice had shaken with the disappointment she had felt because he had not been as amenable or as understanding as she had hoped he would have been, 'I'd thought that you of all people would understand,' she had finished forlornly.

'I understand all right,' Dugald had replied jeeringly. 'I understand that you don't love me or anyone else. You love only yourself, and when you married me, you lied too. You had no intention of keeping the vows you made. You married me to keep in with Hunter so that he would remember you in his will. You married me because your mother said you ought to.'

'Oh, you. . . !' Her temper had boiled over and she had seized a book which had been lying on the bedside table and had hurled it across the room at him. With a rustle of pages it had thudded against the door, just missing him. Immediately sorry for her action, Elizabeth had held her breath, waiting for him to laugh at her as he had always done when she had lost her temper with him. But he hadn't laughed. Bending swiftly, he had picked up the book and had hurled it back at her, and his aim being better than hers, she had been forced to duck to avoid being hit by it. When she had straightened up she had stared at him warily, suddenly afraid of him. He hadn't moved but had returned her stare, his eyes like chips of ice, his mouth curling contemptuously.

'You've just shattered another of my illusions about you,' he had jeered. 'I've always assumed that as a librarian you would treat books with reverence and not throw one in a temper tantrum. Now I know you don't care for books any more than you care for me!'

Opening the door, he had left the room. Elizabeth had slid off the bed and had dressed hurriedly, her mind in turmoil. She had hardly been able to believe that what had happened had actually happened to herself and Dugald. It was the sort of quarrel that happened between other young couples who hadn't been married very long. *They* had the arguments which led to separation or divorce, not she and Dugald, and she had been sure that he would have recovered his temper by the time he joined her at the breakfast table and would have made some humorous remark. She had been sure all would have been forgiven and forgotten.

Looking back now she could see she had behaved more like a spoilt child than an adult woman by expecting him to make the first move and treat her as he had always treated her until then, generously agreeing to let her have her own way and taking back what he had said about separation, smoothing her easily ruffled temper with love-talk and caresses.

But he had not spoken all through breakfast and, bewildered by his silent contempt, she had been unable to find words to bridge the gulf which had widened every minute between them. At last, unable to stand the strain any longer, she had collected up her used dishes and had carried them to the sink.

'I must go or I'll be late for work,' she had said, going towards the door of the flat.

'This is it then?' Dugald had asked, following her. 'You've decided what it is you want to do?'

She had turned to face him and if there had

been any sign of softening in his face she knew
now that she would have flung her arms about
him and would have said she wanted to go with
him to Canada. But his face had been set in hard
unforgiving lines and his eyes had glittered with
hostility. She had remembered then what Fiona
had told her about the woman in Montreal and it
had flashed through her mind that perhaps he
hadn't really wanted her to go with him to
Canada. It had seemed to her that he had agreed
too easily to let her have her own way, had
possibly provoked her into quarrelling with him
so he could suggest a separation. Hating him
suddenly because she believed he could have been
deceiving her ever since they had been married,
she had tilted her head back proudly.

'Yes, I have decided,' she had replied. 'I'm
going to stay here and we'll separate for a while.
As you've said, it will probably suit both of us
very well since neither of us married for love.
Goodbye, Dugald.'

All through that day she had hoped he hadn't
left Brancaster and that she would have found him
at the flat when she had returned in the evening,
but he hadn't been there. Only his plate and a
coffee mug still on the breakfast table and the
rumpled state of the bed had shown that he had
been there with her that morning and the previous
night. Hurting deeply, still finding it hard to believe that their marriage had come to grief so soon,
she had begun to make the bed and tidy the bedroom automatically.

It had been while she had been taking the waste
paper basket from the bedroom to the kitchen to

empty it into the garbage bin that she had noticed two envelopes addressed in strange handwriting in it. She had taken them out and had looked at them. One had contained a letter from a business acquaintance of Dugald's in Canada. The other had contained a letter written in French and had been signed: *Michèle*.

CHAPTER THREE

'Do you know if Hunter changed his will before he died?' Dugald's voice interrupted Elizabeth's flashback thoughts and she turned to look at him.

'No, I don't,' she replied.

'When I saw him last September he was threatening to change it if we didn't get our act together and end our separation,' he said, glancing sideways at her. 'I thought he might have threatened you in the same way.'

'He did say once that he wouldn't leave anything to either of us in his will if we weren't reconciled before he died,' she answered.

'But his threat had no effect on you.'

'Not really. I told him that money ... or the promise of money ... can't buy love,' she said coolly.

'You were speaking only for yourself, of course,' he remarked dryly.

'Of course. But it seems his threat had no effect on you either because you made no move towards a reconciliation.'

'How do you know I didn't?' he retorted, and she glanced at him sharply. His face was dark and unreadable as he kept his glance on the road ahead.

'You made no attempt to contact me when you were over here last September and you haven't written to me all the time we have been

50

separated,' she replied.

Dugald didn't say anything immediately, his attention being given to driving round a particularly severe bend in the road while two cars were coming in the opposite direction. When the road straightened out again he answered her slowly and thoughtfully.

'I'm not a good letter-writer and have never been fond of writing, as you should know, but I did try to see you last September. After all, the two years were up then.'

'What two years?' Elizabeth queried.

'The two years we had agreed to be separated while you studied for that further degree. Hunter told me you got it, by the way. Congratulations.'

'Thank you. Where did you try to see me?'

'I went to Brancaster. You weren't at your flat, so I called at the library. You weren't there either and I was told you were out of the country on a tour of university libraries in France and Germany and that you wouldn't be back until October. I couldn't wait until you returned because I had to fly back to Montreal for a business meeting, so I left a message for you. Didn't you get it?'

'No!' She was very surprised and it showed in the way she exclaimed. 'Where did you leave it?'

'At the library, with another librarian who was on duty at the front desk. He was a thin fair guy, youngish. I think his name was Fawley. He told me where you'd gone and asked me if he could give you a message.'

'He must have forgotten to give it to me,' she muttered, staring wide-eyed at the road in front of her but not seeing it; seeing instead Alan Fawley's narrow pale face. He must have forgotten, she insisted silently to herself. Surely he wouldn't have deliberately withheld from her the information that Dugald had been to see her?

'I had a feeling he might forget,' Dugald said acidly. 'I also got the impression he didn't approve of me and that the relationship between him and you was a bit more than that of fellow librarians. He conveyed the idea to me that you and he were more than friends.'

'Alan has been kind and helpful to me,' she replied stiffly. 'Without his advice and assistance I would never have got my degree, nor would I have been encouraged to apply for the position I have now in the library.'

'That figures,' Dugald drawled. 'He looked the sort of intellectual snob who would encourage a woman to believe she could fulfil her potential better by spending hours cataloguing books and comparing old texts of some obscure, unheard-of, mostly unread literary works than she could by being married and having children.'

'That's sheer prejudice on your part,' she retorted. 'You know nothing about the work a librarian does.'

'I can guess at it,' he said dryly, then added with a wicked flashing grin, 'But you're not going to say I know nothing about women, are you?'

'Oh, I'm sure you know a lot about a certain sort of woman,' she sniped. 'The sort who's happy to stay at home cleaning and decorating, washing and cooking, bathing babies and putting them to bed as long as the man in her life comes home at the end of the day and takes her to bed with him.'

'Now that's what's known as being bitchy, Liz,' he rebuked her. 'Or perhaps I should call you prejudiced too. You've made up your mind, haven't you, to put down any woman who does what you seem to be incapable of doing?'

'No, I haven't. I don't put other women down.' She was fast losing her cool again, over-reacting to his needling remarks. 'Anyway, isn't that what you're doing, putting Alan down, just because he doesn't project a macho image, because he prefers to work indoors and deal with books. You met him only once, yet you dare to judge him.'

'Well, he met me only once and he dared to judge me,' he retorted. 'He more or less told me that he didn't think I was good enough for you and suggested that the sooner you divorced me the better.'

'He didn't?' she gasped.

'He did—and if you don't believe me why don't you ask him the next time you see him? Of course, you might find he'll deny all knowledge of my visit to the library, that he's forgotten I was there, in the same way that he forgot to give you the message,' he sneered.

Her breast heaving, Elizabeth sat in silence, trying to imagine the meeting between Dugald and Alan. It would be like a meeting between a black bear and a sleek greyhound, she thought fancifully, and she could imagine Dugald's forth-right yet domineering manner had irritated the polite, gentle Alan. Dugald must have got under Alan's skin in much the same way that he got under hers, aggravating Alan until he had retaliated.

'You take the right fork here to go into the town,' she said as they approached the outskirts of Duncraig. 'The lawyer's offices are in the Town Hall building on the left side of the High Street.'

'I remember,' said Dugald shortly as he changed gear to go round a roundabout. 'I've been here before, you know.'

'I thought you might have forgotten.'

'Unlike your friend Fawley I never forget . . . *anything*,' he replied tartly.

Past several modern bungalows set in pretty well cared for gardens they drove, then the road narrowed between terraced granite cottages, built long ago, each one with two plain downstairs windows on either side of a plain front door and with two dormer windows poking up from their grey slate roofs.

'I wish I'd known you'd been to see me at Brancaster,' Elizabeth said, watching the cottages give way to small shops.

'But you must have known. Hunter must have told you that I'd gone there to see you. He knew I was going there when I left Nethercraig,' he said. 'Didn't he tell you?'

'Yes, he told me . . . but I didn't believe him,' she muttered. 'You see . . . not knowing that you'd gone to see me because I didn't get your message, I assumed you must have lied to Hunter just to mollify him and to stop him from grumbling to you about our separation.'

'I had no idea you had such a low opinion of me,' he said stingingly. 'In all the years I knew him I didn't lie to Hunter once. He wasn't the sort of person you could lie to.'

'I'm sorry,' she said stiffly. 'I believe you now. What did you say in the message you left?'

'I said that I'd been to see you, was sorry to have missed you, and I asked you to write to me to tell me what you wanted to do; whether you wanted to end the separation or extend it,' he replied coolly.

'And what did you think when I didn't write?' she asked hesitantly.

They had reached the centre of the town where a war memorial, a Celtic cross made from grey granite, stood at the junction of four streets. Behind the cross on a corner was the Town Hall, which was also built of the same sparkling grey stone, and the hands on the clock in the tower indicated that it was five minutes past two. They were late for the appointment.

'I assumed that you wanted the separation to continue,' said Dugald, turning in his seat to look over his shoulder as he reversed the car neatly into a space between two other cars parked at the kerbside. He switched off the engine and turned to look at Elizabeth. His eyes were as grey as the granite and about as hard.

'You . . . you could have written to me again,' she rebuked him.

'Ever heard of pride?' he retorted. 'I'd made my move and as far as I was concerned the next move was yours. How was I to know your boy-friend in the library had other ideas?'

'I'm sure Alan wouldn't interfere deliberately,' she said defensively.

'And I'm pretty sure he would,' he retorted. 'And did.' He paused, lashes veiling his eyes, mouth twisting bitterly. 'If Hunter hadn't died this week I wouldn't be here now having this conversation with you. I'd made up my mind, you see, when I didn't hear from you, that I wasn't coming to see you again unless you asked me to come.' He turned and opened the door. 'And now let's go in and find out if Hunter carried out his threat and cut us both out of his will,' he added tautly.

The offices of Bothwell, Bothwell and Lamont were on the second floor of the Town Hall building and were reached by a flight of stairs covered in brown linoleum which squeaked under the soles of their shoes. In the first room they entered they were greeted by a middle-aged woman. When they told her they were there to see Mr Ian Bothwell she informed them sharply that they were almost ten minutes late and directed them down a passageway to the first door on the left.

Mr Ian Bothwell, the senior partner in the firm of solicitors, was a short man with sparse grey hair. Extremely well-mannered, he rose to his feet as soon as they entered his book-lined room and came round the desk to shake hands with them. He pushed two chairs towards the desk and asked them both to sit down, then he returned to his own chair on the other side of the desk.

'I'm very glad you were able to come, Mr Morin,' he said. 'Without your presence here it would have been difficult for us to carry out the terms of Mr Finley's will. He named you the chief executor and trustee.'

'What does that mean?' asked Dugald, taking off his parka before he sat down.

'It means you have to make sure all the bequests are made and you have to fill out and sign the papers for probate.'

'Probate?' asked Elizabeth. 'What's that?'

'It's the proving of the will by a special court. Once we've estimated the value of the bequests and made sure that the people to whom they have been made are able to receive them we submit the will to the court for verification, so that death duties can be assessed,' replied Mr Bothwell. 'Now, I've had copies of the will made, one for each of you, and I would like you to read it through. When you've done that we can discuss it.'

The will began by naming Dugald as chief executor. From that statement it went on to list the bequests of small amounts of money or items from his collection of antiques and original paintings that Hunter had made to various friends, to his housekeeper, his chauffeur and his gardener. The biggest and most important bequests were last on the list and involved only Elizabeth and Dugald.

To them he had left the house known as Nethercraig, the freehold land surrounding it and the small island of Mindoon with its cottage to hold in trust for the eldest male child born to them. In the event of a male child not being born the property was to descend to their eldest female child. With the property he had left a sizeable annuity to be used for its upkeep. He had also left to them the residue of his estate, mostly shares in various companies, to be shared equally between them after the payment of all debts and expenses relating to his funeral.

Elizabeth and Dugald finished reading the will at the same time and looked across at Mr Bothwell.

'Does it seem straightforward to you?' he asked.

'According to the date this is the will he made soon after Liza and I were married,' Dugald said. 'So he didn't change it.'

'No, he didn't change it.' Mr Bothwell looked suddenly very uncomfortable. In fact Elizabeth thought he blushed and he actually ran a finger round the inside of his crisp shirt collar as if he found it too tight. 'At this point I have to ask you both if you're still married to each other,' he said in a rather choked voice.

His black eyebrows tilting in sardonic surprise, Dugald looked across at Elizabeth.

'Yes, I believe we are still married, aren't we, Liza?'

'Yes,' she murmured.

'But you've been living separately for the last two and a half years, according to Mr Finley,' said Mr Bothwell, and frowned rather severely as if he didn't approve of such behaviour. 'Are you still separated?'

There was an uncomfortable tense silence for about a minute. Again Dugald looked across at Elizabeth. This time a faint mocking smile curved his mouth.

'No,' he said coldly and clearly. 'The separation ended today when I arrived in Kilford, and we intend to stay married, don't we, Liza?' The glance he gave her was bright and challenging.

He had put her on the spot deliberately, knowing that she wouldn't like to answer such a direct personal question in front of a third party who happened to be a lawyer. After giving him a scathing glance she looked across at Mr Bothwell.

'At the moment we haven't done anything to end our marriage,' she said, coolly noncommittal. 'Why do you ask?'

Mr Bothwell looked even more troubled. Picking up his copy of the will, he turned over the top two pages and stared down at a third page.

'Mr Finley was very concerned lately about the state of your marriage in so far as it affected his will, so he asked me to draw up a codicil . . . that is an addition to the original will modifying it or revoking it . . . should the circumstances have changed. That's why I had to ask you both if you're still married, because if you're not married or if there's any possibility of a divorce this codicil comes into effect.'

'You'd better tell us what it says,' said Dugald flatly, and Mr Bothwell cleared his throat and looked uncomfortable again.

'It says that in the event of your separation continuing and ending in a divorce the bequests made to you both in the will are to be cancelled and everything, the property and all the shares, are to be sold and the money left to Mr Finley's favourite charity.'

There was another silence, broken only by the click-clack of a typewriter being used in the next room. Then Dugald laughed. Elizabeth turned to him.

'It isn't funny!' she flared, something she always seemed to be saying to him, she thought.

'I think it is, in an ironic sort of way,' he retorted. 'It's very clever too. Hunter was a wily old bird.' He glanced across at Mr Bothwell. 'What do we do now?'

'Well, as the chief executor you have to do your best to see that the terms of the will are carried out,' replied the lawyer. 'You must find all the pieces of furniture, jewellery and the paintings listed in the first bequests and make sure that the people to whom they've been left receive them. The same with the bequests of money.'

'And what about the bequests of the property which involve myself and my wife? What do I do about them?'

'It's all very difficult,' sighed Mr Bothwell. 'You see, I have only your word that you're intending to stay married.' He gave Dugald an apologetic glance.

'You mean we could lie to you, say that we intend to stay married just to get the loot and once we have it in our possession we could split?' Dugald said in his blunt way.

'Exactly,' said Mr Bothwell, who was actually perspiring with discomfort and embarrassment. 'I warned Mr Finley when he insisted on having the codicil drawn up that he would be putting you both in a difficult position.'

'I would like to make it clear that when Mr Morin says we could lie to you and say we intend to stay married just so we can inherit the property and the shares, he's speaking for himself and not for me,' said Elizabeth spiritedly. 'I would never lie so that I could benefit from the will.'

'I'm very relieved to hear you say so, Mrs Morin,' Mr Bothwell said, smiling and nodding at her. 'But I'm afraid that in this case your word is not going to be enough. I feel that I must still protect my client's wishes, and so before we go any further with the settling of the will and to make it easier for Mr Morin as the executor I would like you both to make a written as well as a verbal statement before witnesses stating that you're still legally married and intend to stay married.'

'Oh, but that would be like getting married all over again!' exclaimed Elizabeth. 'And I'm not sure. . . .'

'Before we agree to do anything like that I think my wife and I should discuss the matter privately.' Just the slightest hint of laughter resounded in Dugald's deep voice.

'Yes, yes, of course,' said Mr Bothwell hastily. 'But I hope you won't be too long making a decision. Meanwhile you could be settling the smaller bequests during the next few days. Suppose we make an appointment to meet again here next Monday at two o'clock? By then I could have a statement drawn up for you to sign and have the appropriate witnesses on hand.'

'Sounds all right to me,' said Dugald, rising to his feet. 'How about you, Liza? Can you be here then?'

'I think so,' she said, also standing up. 'We'll let you know if for some reason we can't come then,' she added, turning to Mr Bothwell who had come round the desk to show them to the door.

'Of course. Ring me any time if you need my advice on anything,' he said.

They were out of the town and on the road to Kilford before Elizabeth gave way and expressed her feelings.

'I think you had a nerve to lie the way you did!' she exploded.

'I lied?' he queried on a note of surprise.

'Yes. When you said our separation ended today and that we intend to stay married.'

'As far as I'm concerned it did end today and I do intend to stay married to you,' he replied coolly. 'So I didn't lie.'

'But you only said that so that Hunter's will could be proved and so that you could get your share of the property and investments,' she retorted.

'And so that you would get your share too,' he reminded her sharply, then added more slowly, 'And so that Hunter would get his wish.' He sighed rather wearily.

'What wish?'

'You know damned well,' he growled at her irritably. 'His wish that both of us should benefit from his will and that the Finley property should be handed down to our child.'

Elizabeth was silent, looking away through the window across the curve of green fields to a lochan, a small lake edged with reeds, twinkling blue and silver in the afternoon sunshine.

It was true, then, what Fiona had told her. Dugald had only married her because he had known he would benefit from Hunter's will if he did. He hadn't married her because he loved her.

Having confirmation of what she had suspected to be true for so long shouldn't have hurt, but it did. She felt thoroughly miserable because he could be so deceitful.

'Well, you needn't think I'm going to say I intend to stay married to you before witnesses,' she said, 'because it wouldn't be true.'

'This is news to me,' he said on a note of surprise. 'Aren't you going to stay married to me?'

'No.'

'And how are you going to become un-married to me?' She could tell by the sound of his voice that he was laughing at her again.

'I . . . I'll divorce you.'

'On what grounds?'

'Oh, I'll find something,' she flared.

Dugald didn't retort, and she didn't say anything else because she was too disturbed by the way divorce had reared its ugly head. She hadn't intended to mention it at all. She frowned in puzzlement at her chaotic thoughts as the car topped the crest of the hill by Kilford church and she had a fleeting glimpse of the island of Mindoon, pink and green seeming to float between the sky and the sea, tied to the mainland by the pale ribbon of shingle and mud, with the uncovered sandbanks of the firth shining silver under the rays of the sun. Then they were turning into the driveway which led to Nethercraig.

'I'm bushed,' yawned Dugald as they entered the hallway. 'Jet-lag, I guess. I think I'll go to bed for a while, catch up on some sleep. See you later.'

She watched him go up the stairs two at a time,

his parka slung over his shoulder. A few moments
later she heard a door close. Slipping off her coat,
she laid it across one of the antique mahogany
hall chairs—heirlooms, she supposed they were
now, to be looked after by Dugald and herself
and passed on to their eldest child . . . if they ever
had a child . . . just to please a romantic, idealistic
old man.

She lifted her hands through her hair as if it
were suddenly too heavy for her head. Oh, God,
what was she going to do? How could she swear
to stay married to Dugald in front of witnesses
knowing that he hadn't married her because he
loved her but because he knew he would benefit
financially from such a marriage, and that once
he had inherited his share of the property and
investments he would probably leave her again?

Going into the kitchen expecting to find Jane
Brodie there she found the room deserted. Jane
must have gone for a walk or perhaps had gone to
visit a friend in the village. Elizabeth sat down at
the table and took out her copy of the will. She
might as well study the small bequests and find
the items listed. She was much more likely to
know where they were than Dugald was because
she had always taken more interest in Hunter's
collections than he had, but she guessed they
might need Jane's help in locating some of the
objects.

An hour later, having found some of the items,
she returned to the kitchen in search of Jane. The
woman wasn't there. Puzzled, because usually at
that time the housekeeper was preparing the
evening meal, Elizabeth went down the passage

to Jane's private room. There was no answer to her knock, so she opened the door and looked into the room. Jane wasn't there and the room had the bare look of having been vacated. There were no personal things scattered about the place and the single bed had been stripped of its sheets. The blankets and bed cover were folded in a neat pile at the end of the bed.

Had Jane left while she and Dugald had been in Duncraig? Elizabeth wondered. But surely she would have left a note. There was no sign of a note in the bedroom and when she returned to the kitchen she could find nothing there. Why had Jane gone? Had she taken offence because they hadn't eaten all the dinner she had prepared?

Suddenly there flashed into Elizabeth's mind the scene at the doorway of the dining room when she had accidentally collided with Jane. Dugald had urged her to go for her coat while he had a word with the housekeeper. Had he told Jane to leave? Had he given her the sack? But he had no right to do that. Or had he?

Going back into the hall, she picked up her coat and went upstairs to put it away in her bedroom. The golden light from the sunset shafted in through the stained glass window at the turn on the stairs, splashing the carpet and woodwork with blobs of blue, green and red light. The landing was already gloomy, so she switched on one of the table lamps. Her room also was full of shadows and she walked across to the dressing table to switch on the lamp there.

She hung her coat in the wardrobe, closed the

door and turned back to the dressing table. As she did she caught sight of two suitcases which had been set down on the floor at the end of the bed. Neither of them belonged to her. Her glance lifted to the bed. Dugald was lying on it under the quilt and he seemed to be fast asleep.

'Oh, really!' she exclaimed, going over to the bedside to glare down at his unconscious face. 'You are the limit! Couldn't you have gone to sleep in another room?'

He didn't hear her, so he didn't answer her. Elizabeth stared down at him. She was very tempted to shake him into wakefulness and insist that he go and sleep elsewhere, but something, a feeling of empathy with his weariness, prevented her. The feeling was like a crack in thick ice and while she stood there looking down at his strong hawkish profile, dark against the pale yellow cotton of the pillowslip, his black hair tousled and falling in all directions, the crack widened and another feeling bubbled up; a feeling of tenderness. Almost she leaned forward to touch him, to stroke her fingers down his cheek and along the tough line of his bristly chin. Almost she knelt down at the bedside so as to be closer to him to touch her lips to his in the hope of awakening him, as she had done so many times when they had slept together.

Then sanity returned. With an exclamation of impatience and irritation with her own weakness she turned away sharply, intending to leave the room, and she had actually taken a step away from the bed when her right hand was caught in a strong grip.

'Don't go,' murmured Dugald, his voice thick with sleep. 'Stay a while.'

'No!' She tried to pull her hand free, but his grip tightened and she was jerked towards the bed. Losing her balance, she fell sideways across him. At once his arms went about her.

'Let me go!' she cried, and pushing against him tried to get up. His arms tightened about her.

'Come to bed,' he whispered, and she felt the tantalising movement of his lips against the hollow at the base of her throat.

'No!' Again she pushed against his bare shoulders in an effort to break free and bent backwards against the steel-like strength of his arms. 'It's too early for me to come to bed. It's only half past six.'

'It's never too early for you and me to go to bed together,' Dugald murmured suggestively, and with a sudden heave of his body beneath hers he tipped her over on to the bed so that she was lying beside him, still trapped by his arms. Pushing up on one elbow, he loomed over her, his tight eyes glinting in his shadowed face.

'I don't want to be in bed with you. I don't want to sleep with you!' she seethed, twisting away from him, only to be stopped by the weight of one of his legs as he thrust it across both of hers. 'And I think you've got a nerve to assume that our separation is over and to come in here to sleep!'

'I came in here to sleep because this is my room and always was when I used to live here. You're the intruder here. The small guestroom was yours, so why haven't you been sleeping in that since you came?' he retorted.

'I . . . oh, because Jane had got this room ready,' Elizabeth blustered. 'And that reminds me—she's gone. All her things have gone. What did you say to her?'

'I told her to take a holiday, starting today,' he replied, his fingers busy at the fastening of her high-necked blouse.

'Why?'

'Because I don't like the way she cooks. She was delighted by the suggestion and asked if she could leave right away to catch the bus to Dumfries. She's been wanting to visit her sister in Edinburgh for some time but wasn't able to leave Hunter.' He grabbed both of her hands which had been fastening the blouse as quickly as he had been unfastening it and his eyes glittered menacingly as he leaned closer to her. 'Listen, if you persist in fastening your blouse I'll be forced to rip it off you,' he purred.

'You wouldn't be so uncivilised,' she taunted spiritedly.

'I could be, very easily,' he threatened, his breath hot against her cheek. 'Deny me my rights and you'll find out just how uncivilised I can be, my tiger lady!'

He dropped her hands suddenly, but before she could move he was on top of her, his mouth swooping to hers. Forgetful of how dangerous it was for her to resist him, she fought, pinching and scratching him, pulling his hair and taking advantage every time he flinched away from her or gasped laughingly with pain to slide from beneath him. But every time she gained the edge of the bed his arms went around her again and she was hauled back to be kissed unmercifully.

As always when she had fought with him in the past, close contact with his bare body, the seductive touch of his fingers as he smoothed her blouse and then her slip from her breasts, aroused her desire, weakening her resistance, and she was going down for the fourth time, swirling round in a vortex of intoxicating sensual delight, when Dugald stiffened and raised his head.

'What is it?' she whispered, her hands sliding over his back luxuriating in the silkiness of skin stretched taut over firm muscles.

'A bell. Didn't you hear it?'

She listened intently through the soft hiss of their combined panting breaths.

'The front door,' she muttered. 'Who can it be?'

'We don't have to answer,' he murmured, his fingers curving about her cheek, turning her face and lips towards his. But the bell rang again loudly and insistently, disturbing both of them.

'I'll go,' said Elizabeth, pushing him away and sitting up. Sliding off the bed, she pulled up her slip straps. Picking up her blouse, she thrust her arms into the sleeves while her feet found and slipped into her discarded shoes.

'You'll come back.' It was a command, not a question, and she gave him a quick glance, before turning and hurrying across to the door as the bell rang again.

'Don't count on it,' she retorted lightly, and left the room to run down the stairs, fastening her blouse as she went. In the hall she switched on the lights, glanced in the oval, gilt-edged mirror to make sure her blouse was decent. Her hair was a wild tangle, her cheeks were flushed and her eyes were sparkling and her lips were ... well, they looked as if they had been very thoroughly kissed. The old-fashioned bell jangled loudly and imperatively above her head.

'Oh, all right, I'm coming!' she muttered, and walked over to the vestibule door. Pulling it open, she stepped out into the coolness of the porch and tugged open the solid front door. Beneath the harsh glare of the outside light two people stood. One was Fiona Edgar and the other was Alan Fawley.

CHAPTER FOUR

ELIZABETH stared in astonishment at the couple standing on the doorstep.

'Hello, Liza,' said Fiona. As always she looked very neat and pretty. Her short brown hair was cut skilfully to curve about her small well-shaped and her triangular face was softly pink and white above the turned-up collar of her blue raincoat, which was exactly the colour of her deep blue eyes. She made Elizabeth very conscious of the wild tangle of her hair and half-fastened blouse hanging loosely outside the waistband of her skirt. 'I was walking along the road, on my way here to see you, when Mr Fawley stopped to ask me the way to Nethercraig. I offered to come with him and show him the way.'

'Hello, Elizabeth,' said Alan, smiling at her. In an oyster-white trenchcoat, belted at the waist, slim and slight, his blond hair smooth, his long narrow face pale, he seemed like a straw that could be blown away in the wind.

'Hello,' she replied rather weakly. Why had he come? The question screeched through her mind. And what on earth was she going to do with him now that he was here? She became aware that while she hesitated the other two were being soaked by the drizzle of rain which had begun to fall. 'Won't you come in?' she said politely, and hoped that she didn't sound too reluctant.

They stepped past her into the hallway and she closed the door. When she turned round Fiona came towards her and kissed her cheek.

'How are you bearing up?' Fiona asked softly, her blue eyes glowing with sympathy. 'I read about Mr Finley's death in the Glasgow paper and guessed you'd be here, so as soon as school finished this afternoon I drove down hoping to see you. You must be feeling very sad. I know how fond of him you were.'

'I am rather upset,' Elizabeth muttered. Trust Fiona to say all the right things at the right time—and yet somehow her friend's sympathy didn't touch her. She turned to Alan. 'I'm sorry you had trouble finding the house,' she said. 'If you'd phoned me before you left Brancaster to tell me you were coming I'd have given you more detailed directions on how to get here.'

'I did phone, but there was no reply, so I set out anyway,' he explained, with the boyish grin which made him so endearing. 'I thought I'd spend the weekend here.' He glanced at Fiona. 'I've not been to this part of the country before,' he added enthusiastically, 'and knowing that Elizabeth was staying here gave me a good excuse to drive up and have a look around.' He looked back at Elizabeth, his sherry-coloured eyes crinkling at the corners as he smiled at her. 'To tell you the truth, love,' he continued, 'I've missed you since you left the library last Tuesday. The hours and days have been quite empty and dull without your presence.'

'It's nice of you to say so,' said Elizabeth as lightly as she could, glancing quickly at Fiona and wondering if she had noticed the endearment Alan had used. Fiona was looking down at the dark leather gloves she was carrying and smoothing the fingers out as if to do so was most important. 'Alan and I work together in the library at Brancaster University,' Elizabeth added hurriedly.

'So he was telling me as we drove here,' replied Fiona, looking up. There was no smile on her face and the expression in her eyes was one of cool speculation.

Elizabeth glanced towards the staircase hoping that Dugald would stay upstairs. Somehow she must persuade her unwelcome visitors to leave before Dugald knew they were in the house.

'Have you had anything to eat?' she asked Alan.

'Not since I left Brancaster,' he said.

'Then I'd like to suggest we go and have dinner together at the Castle Craig Hotel. I'd offer you a meal here, but Jane the housekeeper has gone away on holiday and there isn't much food in the house. The hotel isn't far away and the meals are very good. Fiona can vouch for that.'

'It sounds like a good idea,' said Alan, much to her relief. 'Perhaps you'd like to join us for dinner?' he added gallantly, turning to Fiona.

'Thank you, I'd like to,' she replied. 'But I think we should phone the hotel first and ask them to reserve a table for us. They get busy on a Friday night.'

'The phone is right there, Fiona,' said Elizabeth, pointing to the hall table. 'If you wouldn't mind making the reservation I'll go up and fetch my coat. You could book a room there for the night at the same time, Alan.'

'Oh, but . . .' he began,

'I'm afraid I can't put you up here,' she whispered, glancing warningly in the direction of Fiona who had turned away to the phone. 'Not without Jane being here. You do understand, don't you?'

'I suppose so,' he muttered, frowning at her. 'Elizabeth, what's the matter with you? You seem on edge for some reason.'

'Oh, nothing, nothing,' she said airily, turning away and hurrying towards the stairs. 'I'll be as quick as I can.'

She dashed up the stairs, colliding with Dugald when she reached the top of the second flight where he had been standing looking over the banisters into the hallway, hidden from sight. His hands caught at her shoulders roughly to steady her and his eyes glittered dangerously as he glared down at her. His hair still tousled, he was dressed only in a three-quarter-length dressing gown.

'That's Fawley down there, isn't it?' he rapped.

'Yes.' She tried to twist free, but he wasn't letting her go.

'What the hell is he doing here?' he demanded. 'Did you invite him to come?'

Remembering that she had often said to Alan that if he was ever in the Kilford district and she happened to be at Nethercraig he should call to see her, she hesitated.

'Er—not exactly,' she muttered, and seeing suspicion flare in Dugald's eyes and his mouth twist cynically she added quickly, 'At least not in the way you mean. I didn't invite him to come and stay here ... this time. Oh, where are you going?' she demanded as, releasing her, he began to go down the stairs.

'I'm going to throw him out,' he retorted.

'No, Dugald ... you mustn't!' She ran after him and tugged at his arm. 'Please don't go down. Fiona is there too ... and ... well, they don't know you're here. All three of us are going out to dinner and she's phoning to make a reservation at Castle Craig Hotel. Oh, Dugald, please don't go down!'

He looked down at her, his eyebrows tilting in quizzical surprise.

'Dinner, eh?' he drawled. 'I wouldn't mind a good square meal myself. Okay, I won't throw your lover-boy out. ...'

'He is not my lover-boy!' Elizabeth seethed.

'I'll go and ask Fiona to make the reservation for four,' he went on, as if she hadn't spoken, and turning quickly ran down the rest of the stairs before she could stop him.

In the bedroom she went straight to the mirror on the dressing table intending to tidy her hair and noticed that her blouse was torn after all, at the front too. The trouble with Dugald was he didn't know his own strength, she fumed as she took the blouse off, and she hoped that neither Fiona nor Alan had noticed the tear, glad that the slip she had been wearing under the sheer black blouse was black too. Searching in the wardrobe for something which was adequately subdued and suitable for mourning wear, she chose a short dress made from silky material patterned in soft greys and violets. She pulled off her skirt and slipped the dress over her head. She was struggling with the zip at the back when Dugald came back into the room. He came right across to her and did up the zip, then began to take off his robe.

'It's all fixed up. I'm coming to dinner too,' he said, bending to one of his open suitcases and taking out a shirt.

'Oh no!' Elizabeth groaned as she tugged a comb through her tangled hair.

'What do you mean by "oh, no"?' he snapped at her, coming to stand behind as he pulled on the shirt so that they could see each other reflected in the mirror. 'I'm hungry, and if you're not going to stay at home to cook a meal I'm coming with you.' He began to fasten the buttons on the shirt and grinned at her tauntingly. 'Besides, you need a fourth in the party to entertain Fiona while you and your lover . . . oops, sorry . . . your librarian friend whisper sweet nothings to each other.'

'Alan and I do not whisper sweet nothings!' she hissed at him. 'And I can't understand why you're so suspicious of my friendship with him.'

'No more than I can understand why you're so suspicious of my friendship with Michèle or any other woman,' Dugald retorted as he pulled on a pair of dark grey worsted trousers. While he belted them he watched her outlining her lips with a pale lipstick. 'Too bad they came when they did,' he said softly when the belt was buckled, and coming closer he slid his arms about her waist, his head bending to the curve where her neck met her shoulders. Against her skin his lips were warm and seductive, and delicious shivers quivered through her. 'The deep frost was thawing nicely,' he whispered. 'Another few minutes and it would have been completely melted.'

'I don't know what you're talking about,' she replied, slipping from between his hands and going over to the wardrobe for her coat, trying to pretend that her heart hadn't increased its beat and that the heat of desire was not flaming through her again.

'I'm talking about what was happening twenty minutes ago on that bed and what would have happened if the doorbell hadn't rung,' Dugald said harshly.

'Oh, you mean when you were asserting your marital rights and overcoming the resistance,' she couldn't help taunting him as she pushed her arms into the sleeves of her coat. In the next instant her elbow was seized by cruelly bruising fingers and she was swung round violently to face him. His face had a savage tautness about it and a livid light glittered in his eyes, like lightning flickering before a thunderstorm.

'It was more than that,' he said between his teeth.

'Was it?' she retorted with mock-sweetness.' I don't think so. It never has been more than physical domination and possession for you.'

'Something which you've enjoyed experiencing,' he retaliated.

'Something I have endured, you mean,' she countered her glance direct, meeting his and challenging him.

His fingers tightened even more cruelly and she

gasped with the pain. He seemed to growl deeply in his throat and again she knew both fear and excitement as she expected him to react violently to her taunting of him. Then his hand left her elbow and his eyes were hidden by their heavy smooth lids as a faintly mocking smile curved his lips.

'Thanks for telling me,' he drawled. 'I would never have guessed from your responses that you were enduring this evening or any of the other times we've made love.'

He turned away and went back to his suitcase to select a tie. Going over to the dressing table, he put the tie under the collar of his shirt and began to knot it, watching himself in the mirror, ignoring her. Made slightly uneasy by his sudden withdrawal, Elizabeth watched him warily. Had she gone too far? Had she hurt his feelings? No, surely not. Dugald was too confident a lover to be hurt by what she had said, too knowledgeable about women's reactions to even believe what she had said. So why had she said it? What had she hoped to achieve? A confession from him that he wanted to make love to her not just because he was physically attracted to her but because she meant more to him than any other woman in the world, because he loved her.

'I'll go and tell the others you won't be long,' she muttered, picking up her handbag and stalking across to the door she left the room.

Fiona and Alan were in the sitting room, standing before an original watercolour which had been painted by a leading English artist of the 1930s and which was now worth a great deal of money. They seemed to be getting on well to-gether and were talking animatedly about the painting, but when they saw her enter the room they stopped.

'I was so surprised to see Dugald,' Fiona enthused, coming across the room.

'Were you really?' remarked Elizabeth dryly. 'But you must have guessed he would come when he heard Hunter had died.'

At that moment Dugald came into the room. He had put on a bluish grey tweed jacket and was carrying his parka. With his powerful physique and dark dynamic good looks he made Alan seem fragile and very youthful.

'I'd like to take my car,' he said, 'so that Elizabeth and I have a vehicle to return here in when the evening is over.'

'Then I'll go with Alan in his car to show him the way to the hotel,' said Elizabeth, thinking it would give her a chance to talk privately with the young man and persuade him to go back to Brancaster the next day.

'And I'll go with you, Dugald,' said Fiona, smiling up at him. 'It's such a long time since you and I had a good talk, almost six months, in fact, when you were visiting Mr Finley last September.'

'You can fill me in all the latest gossip,' replied Dugald, turning to her with one of his most be-guiling smiles, and Fiona pushed her hand through the crook of his arm as they went towards the door.

As if it were her right to go with him instead of mine, thought Elizabeth acidly as she felt jealousy corkscrew through her, and turning to Alan she pushed her arm through his.

'We'll go first,' she said in an over-loud voice. 'I've such a lot to tell you, Alan.'

Alan's car was parked right in front of the house, so they were soon sitting in it and driving towards the road.

'Turn left at the end of the drive,' she said to him. 'And just follow the road. The Castle Craig Hotel is on the right on a hill overlooking the Firth. It's a house not unlike Nethercraig and was built by a Scottish industrialist at the end of the last century as his country residence. A few years ago the Arnotts bought it and turned it into a hotel. It's supposed to be on the site of an old Iron Age hill fort, which might interest you.'

'Any excavations ever done there?' Alan asked. His favourite spare-time occupation was amateur archaeology.

'I don't know. Fiona might be able to tell you about that. She teaches history.'

'I thought she seemed very knowledgeable,' Alan said approvingly. He never hid his preference for well-informed, intelligent women. 'She's good-looking, too.'

'Yes, I suppose she is,' replied Elizabeth vaguely, and felt again the sharp twist of jealousy she had experienced when Dugald had smiled at Fiona and the woman had responded. So they had met last September, had they? Where? Here? Or had Dugald gone up to Glasgow? Oh, what did it matter? She wasn't in love with Dugald any more, so she shouldn't feel jealous just because he had smiled at Fiona in that beguiling way as if he hoped to revive their close friendship.

'It must be difficult for you, having Morin staying in the same house, considering you and he are separated,' Alan commented.

'He has assumed that the separation is over,' she replied coolly.

'But surely you haven't agreed to end it?' he exclaimed, half turning to her, taking his glance off the road, and the car swerved alarmingly on the wet surface.

'Oh, do watch what you're doing, Alan!' she exclaimed. 'The ditches are quite deep here and I wouldn't like your car to fall into one. In another quarter of a mile you'll see the entrance to the driveway to Castle Craig. There's a sign with a light over it.'

'You haven't answered my question,' he complained, as he looked ahead of him again, hunching over the steering wheel in his usual nervous fashion. 'Have you agreed to end the separation?'

'No, I haven't.'

'Thank God,' he whispered.

'Not yet, anyway.'

'Not yet? Does that mean you're thinking about ending it?' he demanded, his voice rising incredulously.

'Yes, I am. I have to,' said Elizabeth.

'Why? Why do you have to?'

'Because . . . oh, it's so difficult to explain. It's because of Hunter's will.'

'Now let me get this straight. Hunter was your cousin. Right?'

'Yes . . . and in his will it states that Nethercraig and his investments are left to Dugald and me as long as we remain married and hold them in trust for our eldest child.'

'Good God!' Alan exclaimed. 'And what happens if you don't remain married?'

'The house and all the investments are to be sold and the money given to Hunter's favourite charity.' Elizabeth paused, then added sadly, 'Hunter must have been awfully disappointed in Dugald and me.'

'Why? What had you done to disappoint him?'

'It was his dearest wish that we should marry and he was very happy when we did, so he must have been disappointed when we separated and that was why he had the codicil to the will drawn up. It was his attempt to reconcile us.'

'If you ask me, he must have been off his rocker if he thought he could dictate how you and Dugald should live,' remarked Alan critically. 'But now I understand your position. There's not much chance of Dugald agreeing to a divorce now, is there? I mean, he'll want to stay married to you to benefit from the will. God, what a fix you're in!'

'Yes, I suppose I am,' said Elizabeth miserably.

'I can see he'll really be applying the pressure,' he said grimly. 'Oh yes, I can see it. He'll be doing his utmost to make you pregnant.' The car swerved again as he glanced at her. 'You can't stay in that house with him, darling—I won't let you. I'm going to rescue you from his clutches and be damned to your cousin's will.'

'What are you going to do?' Elizabeth exclaimed as he put his foot down on the accelerator.

'Oh, you've gone past the hotel. Alan, slow down, please. You'll have to find a place to turn so we can go back.'

'I'm not going back. I'm going to take you away with me tonight,' Alan retorted excitedly, changing down noisily as the road dipped down steeply. Below them, flickering through the trees, were the lights of Kilford, blurred by the drizzle.

'But what about the others, Dugald and Fiona? They'll wonder where we've gone,' said Elizabeth. 'Alan, please slow down and go back!'

'No. What's this place we're coming to?'

'Kilford.' Elizabeth closed her eyes as the car slithered and slid at a dangerously fast speed down the steep hill to the road which wound along beside the estuary. She was convinced that the brakes would fail at the bottom of the hill and they would charge right across the narrow road and into the marshes. But miraculously the brakes held and the car came to a sudden jolting stop beside the small general store and post office.

'Where does this road lead to?' asked Alan.

'It goes right through the village and then turns up another hill and joins the main road to Duncraig,' said Elizabeth. 'But you can turn here and go back the way we came to Castle Craig.'

'Not on your life! We're going on to Duncraig and then after that to the next town. We're going as far away from Dugald Morin as we can,' declared Alan determinedly. 'He's not going to compromise you so he can benefit from your cousin's will and so that you can't divorce him— I'll see to that!'

While he was talking Alan put the car in gear

and drove past the row of gabled, whitewashed cottages of the village. Sitting beside him, speechless with amazement at his behaviour, Elizabeth wondered what she could do to stop him from kidnapping her, because that was what he was doing. To grab his arm in an attempt to make him stop the car again would be dangerous and might cause an accident. The only way she could think of was to talk him into taking her back.

'I'm really very hungry,' she said. 'And I was looking forward to having a meal at the Castle.'

'We'll stop somewhere along the road to eat. There's bound to be another hotel with a restaurant somewhere. What's the next town after Duncraig?'

'It depends on which way you go. If you go east you'll come to Dumfries. If you go west you'll reach Castle Douglas eventually.'

'We'll go west,' he said, and the car surged confidently up the hill away from Kilford.

'But I don't want to go away with you,' she complained. 'And you have no right to carry me off like this!'

'I'm doing it to help you,' he insisted. 'I'm rescuing you from that bully.'

'Dugald isn't a bully,' she retorted, forgetful that only recently she had accused Dugald of using his superior physical strength to dominate and possess her. 'But if you believe he is aren't you afraid he'll come after us and beat you up for kidnapping his wife?'

'He won't come after us because he won't know where we've gone, and also because your friend Fiona will see to it that he doesn't follow us.'

'What do you mean?'

'Once she's got him to herself she'll make sure he doesn't leave her side. She's in love with him. Hadn't you noticed? And I got the impression from the way he looked at her and talked to her when he came downstairs the first time that he's pretty keen on her. Have they known each other long?'

'Yes, for several years,' she replied tonelessly. She looked away out of the window at the dark drenched outlines of the countryside, but all she saw was Dugald smiling at Fiona and Fiona smiling back at him and putting her hand through the crook of his arm as if he belonged to her. 'They used to go about together a lot before Hunter asked Dugald to marry me,' she added.

'They were having an affair, then?' queried Alan.

'I suppose they were,' she muttered.

'And knowing that, didn't it strike you as strange when Morin asked you to marry him?'

'No, I didn't find it strange,' she replied weakly, remembering the passion which had blazed between herself and Dugald in the cottage on the island of Mindoon. She had been so sure his emotions had been involved, so sure he had been in love with her as much as she had been in love with him. Only a year later she had questioned his sincerity, and only then because of what Fiona had told her, that Dugald had married her to benefit from Hunter's will.

'Did your cousin really ask Morin to marry you?' asked Alan.

'He advised him to.'

'My God, he must have been crazier than I first thought he was! And did he advise you to marry Dugald?'

'No . . . I mean, not obviously. He made it clear that it would please him if we married. He told me he wanted to make sure that the property would descend to someone with Finley blood in their veins.'

'Then he could have left the lot to you and cut Dugald out completely.'

'But he didn't want to do that, because Dugald was his adopted son as well as his stepson and he was very fond of him,' Elizabeth defended. 'I don't think he was nutty. He was just trying to do the best for us.'

'So he messed up both your lives. An arranged marriage!' Alan laughed jeeringly. 'I thought that sort of thing went out of fashion years ago. What a pity your cousin didn't live a little longer. If he'd lived another six or seven months you would have been divorced and then the codicil you've mentioned would have applied immediately.'

Elizabeth didn't reply. Slumped down in her seat, she continued to stare out at the darkness, no longer caring where Alan was taking her. Perhaps if she did as he had suggested, and stayed the night with him somewhere instead of returning to Nethercraig, it would convince Dugald more than any words that she didn't want to stay married to him so that she could benefit from Hunter's will. Perhaps he would realise at last that she wasn't cold and practical like him, and that she couldn't stay married to him knowing he didn't really love her and was quite capable of staying married to her even though he was in love with another woman.

Her thoughts flitted back two and a half years to the day of their first wedding anniversary. Once again she was in the sitting room at Nethercraig with Fiona. How bitter Fiona had been! At the time Elizabeth hadn't understood why, and when Fiona had referred to Dugald as being in love with 'someone else' she had believed Fiona had been referring to the woman in Montreal. Now she realised Fiona had been referring to herself. And then, driven possibly by jealousy and spite, the schoolteacher had blurted out that Dugald had told her his marriage to Elizabeth had been arranged by Hunter. The seed of distrust and suspicion had been sown in Elizabeth's mind, as Fiona had hoped perhaps, and separation from Dugald had followed.

How often had Fiona and Dugald met during the past two and a half years? Was the meeting last September the only one? Or had they met secretly, perhaps in Canada? Fiona could easily have gone on holiday to that country and met him there.

She would never know if they had met more than once, but she didn't want to know. The once was enough, and after meeting Fiona and talking with her he had gone to Brancaster to see herself. To put an end to their separation, he had said. How? By a divorce?

'Dugald says he tried to see me last September and left a message for me with you at the library,' she said. 'Did he?'

'Yes, he came to the library, but he didn't leave

any message for you.' Alan leaned forward to peer through the windscreen as if he wasn't sure of the way, then changing gear he guided the car round the roundabout where the road divided outside Duncraig and drove along the short bypass which led to the main road to Castle Douglas.

'Why didn't you tell me he'd been to the library?' she asked.

'I forgot,' he replied frankly. 'In fact I didn't remember until he came down the stairs at Nethercraig today and I recognised him. He was damned rude when he came to the library. He was furious because you weren't there. I remember telling him that just because you were married to him you didn't have to be at his beck and call.'

'You also told him that he wasn't good enough for me,' observed Elizabeth.

'Yes, I believe I did,' Alan sounded quite pleased with himself.

'You had no right to say that to him,' she rebuked him.

'Well, he made me see red, turning up out of the blue like that demanding to see you as if you were one of his possessions. And I think it was then I realised how much I'd fallen in love with you. I remember now I was quite glad you were away and wouldn't be back before he had to leave.'

'You remember so much I'm surprised you forgot to tell me he had been to see me,' she said tartly. 'You deliberately forgot to tell me, and you deliberately destroyed his message, didn't you? How could you, Alan?'

'All's fair in love and war, darling,' he replied with a nervous little laugh. 'Do you think we're on the right road, by the way? It seems very narrow and twisted.'

'Did you turn left when we came to the end of the Duncraig bypass?'

'No. I went straight on.'

'Then you'd best stop and turn to go back the way we came,' she urged. 'We're probably on a road that goes nowhere.'

'Oh, come on, Elizabeth, if it's a road it must go somewhere,' he argued laughingly. 'And I can't possibly turn yet. There isn't room.'

'It's only a single track,' she said, peering out of the window. 'There's no room to pass anything that might come the other way. It's probably a farm road, leading to one of the farms on the moors behind Duncraig. I wish you'd back up, Alan. It looks awfully muddy. We might get stuck.'

'Not in this,' he replied confidently. 'It has a front-wheel drive.'

'Alan, please will you do as I ask!' she flared suddenly, her voice sharp, 'and reverse down the lane before we get stuck.'

'Now, now, darling, don't get bossy,' he rebuked her, pulling hard on the steering wheel to bring the car round a bend. Immediately ahead of them headlights glared, dazzling both of them.

'There's something coming,' said Elizabeth. 'Now you'll have to reverse.'

Breathing hard, Alan groped for the gear-shift and ground it into reverse. With a roar the car shot backwards, hit something hard, bounced forward, and tipped over on to its side. Alan collapsed against the steering wheel and Elizabeth slid sideways to fall against him.

She didn't actually lose consciousness, but for a few moments she lay inert, dazed by shock and whiplash. Vaguely she was aware of light shining brilliantly through the cracked windscreen from the headlamps of the other vehicle. Doors slammed and there were voices, both of them male. The door above her was opened and a head in a tweed cap appeared.

'How are ye in there?' asked a voice thickened by a broad Scottish accent.

'I . . . I'm not sure,' Elizabeth gasped. 'My . . . my friend seems to have been knocked out.'

'Can ye move your legs and arms without pain?' asked the voice.

She tried moving and found that she could without any difficulty, although when she tried to reach the open door she slid backwards again.

'Yes, I can move, but I don't seem to be able to get out.'

'If ye're quite sure you havena' damaged anything, I'll be giving ye a hand,' replied the man. 'I'm Hamish MacClellan from Knockabie Farm. And who might ye be?'

'Elizabeth Morin. We . . . we . . . missed the turning on to the road and came up here by mistake. We were trying to reverse back down the lane. What did we hit?'

'Ach, ye collided with the big rock. Ye backed right into it, so ye did, instead of taking the bend in the road. Now I'm going to put me hands under your armpits and lift ye up a wee bit.'

Within a few minutes she was out of the car and standing beside her rescuer, feeling dizzy and somewhat bruised.

'Did ye find that torch, Jock?' shouted Hamish MacClellan to the other person who was still in the other vehicle, which was a Ford van.

'Aye, I've got it,' shouted Jock, and jumping out of the van came towards them. He was a boy of about sixteen. He handed the torch to Hamish.

'And now I'll be having a wee look at your friend,' said Hamish, returning to the car and shining the torch inside. 'Well now, he isna' dead, but I doubt we should move him,' he said, returning to Elizabeth. 'Jock, you stay here with the car and I'll take this young lady back to the farm with me and phone the police. This way, Miss Morin. Can ye manage now, all right?'

With an ease born of knowledge of his own road Hamish turned the van and drove back the way he had come. Soon lights appeared, twinkling through the misty drizzle. The van was stopped in a farmyard and Hamish came round to help Elizabeth out. With a helping hand under her elbow he guided her towards the back door of a tall gabled farmhouse.

'The wife has been away all day, shopping in Dumfries,' he explained as he took her into a big kitchen where a fire leapt in an old-fashioned fireplace complete with built-in oven. 'Jock and I were just going down to Duncraig to meet her off the bus. Sit ye down here, lass, by the fire, while I phone the police. They won't take long to get here and they'll arrange for an ambulance to come and take your friend and yourself to the hospital.'

'Thank you,' whispered Elizabeth, and sank down on the edge of the cushioned seat of a ladderbacked rocking chair. She was shaking all over, she discovered, and her nose had begun to bleed. She fumbled in her coat pocket for a handkerchief, listening to the rumble of Hamish's voice coming from the other side of a door which presumably led to the hallway of the house.

'So that's done,' he said when he came back into the room. 'They're on their way now. Will ye be all right, lass, if I leave ye here by yourself and go down to the car to meet them?'

'Yes, I think so. Could I . . . would you mind if I used your phone?' she asked. 'I think it would be a local call to Kilford.'

'Aye, go ahead. The phone is there in the hall. I'll be back soon enough, I expect, with a bobby. He'll be wanting to ask you a few questions.'

He went out and she heard the van start up and drive away. Dabbing at her nose with her handkerchief, she went out into the hall and picked up the receiver. Where should she try first? Castle Craig Hotel or Nethercraig? Where would Dugald be?

She dialled the hotel first. After the phone at the other end of the line had rung a few times it was answered and she recognised Marjorie Arnott's voice.

'Mrs Arnott, this is Elizabeth Morin speaking.'

'Ach, wherever have ye got to?' exclaimed the woman, and Elizabeth could visualise her pink, plump face wearing an anxious expression. 'Mr Morin and Miss Edgar have just this minute left to go and look for ye.'

'Oh. I was hoping to tell Dugald where I am,' said Elizabeth, a desire to burst into tears sweeping over her. 'Do you know where they were going to look?' she asked, her voice not much more than a whisper.

'They said they would go towards Kilford. They thought you must have missed the turning into the drive here. Are you all right, Mrs Morin?'

'I . . . er . . . well, we've been in an accident and we'll be going to the hospital. If my husband comes back to the hotel or contacts you to find out if I've turned up there would you tell him what has happened, please?'

'Yes, of course I will. I hope you're all right and not badly hurt.'

'No, I'm not badly hurt, just shaken up. You can tell Dugald that if he calls.'

She hung up and walked slowly back to the kitchen, thankful to sit down again. Leaning back in the rocker, she watched the flames leaping in the fire and slowly the tears gathered in her eyes and slid down her cheeks. If only she had been able to talk to Dugald and explain everything to him directly. If only he had been at the hotel and not out somewhere with Fiona. Was he really looking for her and Alan?

Poor Alan! She hoped he wasn't seriously injured. It was all her fault that they had been on the narrow farm road. If she hadn't been so taken up with her own bitter thoughts about Fiona and Dugald she would have noticed when they had come to the end of the bypass and would have directed him on to the right road.

No, it went back farther than that. It went back almost two and a half years to those few months after she and Dugald had separated. Lost and unhappy because Dugald had left her, wallowing in misery because she had found out he didn't love her, her confidence in herself destroyed, she had lapped up the attention Alan had given her. Youthful, amusingly absentminded and highly intellectual, he had treated her as a person rather than as a woman and it had been easy to become friendly with him.

But she should never have let him fall in love with her. She should have kept him at a distance. He wouldn't have driven up to see her today if she had and the accident wouldn't have happened. Oh, it was all her fault!

CHAPTER FIVE

SUNLIGHT, butter-yellow, slanted through the windows of the hospital ward where Elizabeth lay resting in bed. It was Saturday afternoon and visitors were beginning to arrive, parents, husbands, wives, boy-friends and girl friends of the few patients who occupied the ward. At first Elizabeth watched the doorway avidly, hoping to see Dugald among the group, but he wasn't there, and after a while she averted her glance and pretended to read the magazine she had been given, not wanting to appear too disappointed because he hadn't come.

The previous evening when she and Alan had been brought in an ambulance to the emergency ward of the hospital the doctor who had examined her had found many bruises and evidence of severe shock and had recommended that she stay in hospital for at least two nights and a day. As soon as the diagnosis had been completed she had been brought on a stretcher to the ward and had been put to bed by a brisk and efficient night nurse.

'I must let my husband know what's happened and where I am,' she had whispered urgently.

'Ach, dinna be worriting your head about that, now. The police will do that. I expect they asked for the name and address of your next of kin, didn't they?' the nurse had replied as she had shaken a large pill out of a phial into the palm of her hand.

'Yes, they did,' The police had asked her many questions and she hoped she had answered them sensibly.

'Then they will inform your husband and tell him when he can come to see you. Now, I want you to take this sleeping tablet. What you need is a good night's rest and you'll be as right as rain in the morning.'

Elizabeth hadn't believed the pill would work, but she had taken it with the water the nurse had offered. She had lain down, the nurse had put off the light and had gone away. For several minutes Elizabeth had stared at the shadowy wall opposite her, listening to the breathing of the sleeping patients, hearing the increased beat of her heart and thinking not of the injured Alan but of Dugald, wondering what he would do when he was informed of the accident, and slowly her tense nerves had relaxed and she had slipped into sleep without knowing it.

This morning when she had been wakened it had taken her some time to realise where she was and what had happened to her. She had eaten some breakfast and then had dozed fitfully until a nurse had come to take her temperature and blood pressure. All morning she had slept off and on and was even tempted to doze off again now. Only the thought that Dugald might come was keeping her awake.

She glanced towards the doorway. No one there. She looked round the ward. Everyone had visitors except her. Would he come? Oh, he must come! She was longing for him to come. She wanted to see his broad-shouldered figure striding towards her more than she wanted anything else in the world. She wanted to see him give her one of his glinting, derisive glances, hear him make some mocking remark. It wouldn't matter what he said to her as long as he put his arms about her and laid his cheek against hers; as long as she experienced again the comfort she knew his strength could give her . . . if she would let it.

But she was also dreading his coming because he might be angry with her for having gone with Alan instead of with him last night. Groaning, she leaned back against the pillow and closed her eyes. Oh, God, why had she been so foolish? Why had she allowed her jealousy of Fiona to govern her actions? If only she could go back in time to the moment when the front door bell had rung yesterday evening she would do everything differently.

She should have done what Dugald had suggested and not answered the door. She should have stayed in bed with him and let what had been going to happen, happen, naturally and joyously, because after all the thaw had almost been completed, the deep frost which had frozen her responses to Dugald had been penetrated and she had been about to give in to her own inflamed desires, to give of herself to him and to take from him what he had been offering. Oh, if only she had done it, if only she had done it! Again she groaned aloud.

'Liza.' Dugald's voice, deep yet crisp, spoke near to her and her eyes flew open.

He was there, standing by the bed, and yet she

hadn't heard him come. Big and vital, casually dressed in jeans, an open-necked checked shirt and the same V-necked Shetland sweater he had worn the day before, he made everyone else in the ward seem puny and underfed. His black hair sprang back from his broad forehead and coiled about his ears and the back of his shirt collar as if it had a life of its own and his olive-tinted skin glowed with good health. As always his physical appearance affected her senses. Her hands itched to touch him, to stroke his skin and ruffle his hair. Her nostrils quivered with the longing to sniff at the earthy male scents of his body and her lips burned with the desire to press against his.

'I'm glad you've come,' she whispered, and stretched out a hand to him, no longer hiding the pleasure that seeing him gave her as she had the previous day.

Dugald didn't take her hand, nor did he move forward to kiss her. Instead he looked round for a chair, found a nurse pushing one towards him, took it, turned it round and straddled it, resting his arms along the back of it. His glance, which was cold and sharp, drifted over her bright hair and her pale face and down to the prim white cotton hospital shift in which she was dressed.

'How are you feeling?' he asked, and there was an unusual cool tone of politeness in his voice.

'Much better than I did last night,' Elizabeth said. 'Although I still ache where I was bruised and my head feels as if it's stuffed with cotton wool, from the sleeping pill they gave me, I think.' She touched fingertips to her temple and laughed a little. 'I hope I make sense when I talk. I might be able to come home tomorrow.'

She was trying to be cool too, but inside she felt raw because Dugald wasn't behaving the way she had hoped he would behave. She had been so sure that gladness because she had survived the accident would have swept aside any anger he had felt and he would have expressed his relief in his usual extravagant way.

'Home?' he repeated, one eyebrow going up in satirical surprise. But derision didn't glint in his eyes. They remained quite cold and empty and his broad-lipped mouth was set in a straight severe line. 'Where's home?'

'Nethercraig,' she whispered, a little shaken by the question. 'Will you come for me tomorrow?'

'I guess so,' he drawled indifferently, lifting his shoulders in one of the shrugs which always reminded her of his French blood. He looked slowly round the ward, inspecting every patient closely, then looked back at her. 'Where's Fawley?' he asked.

'In another ward. He has concussion and a broken leg,' she replied.

'Does he have any relatives who have to be informed he's been hurt and is in hospital?' he asked.

'Yes—his parents. They've been told. The ward Sister told me they're driving up to see him today and will probably make arrangements to have him moved to a hospital near Brancaster.'

'Good. I'm glad I don't have to take the responsibility for him as well as for you,' Dugald said caustically, and she flinched as if he had stabbed her.

'That isn't a kind thing to say,' she rebuked him.

'But I'm not feeling particularly kind today,' he retorted. 'I was up half the night searching for you and Fawley.'

'But surely the police let you know where I was!' Elizabeth exclaimed. 'I was told they would.'

'They did. But I didn't get the message until I got back to Nethercraig at some unearthly hour this morning after having driven nearly as far as Stranraer and back, looking for a car in a ditch or with a flat tyre or run out of petrol,' he said dryly. 'What the hell do you think you were doing, going off with Fawley like you did? Whose idea was it to drive off into the night without warning? His or yours?'

'His. But I didn't know he was going to drive past Castle Craig when I decided to go with him,' she explained. 'He ... he kidnapped me.'

'Really?' he mocked. 'Expect me to believe that?'

'Yes, because it's true,' she flared. 'He didn't want me to stay with you at Nethercraig.'

'Why not?'

'Because ... oh, because he doesn't like you. I asked him to stop and go back to the hotel, but he wouldn't.' She looked at him quickly. His upper lip was curling contemptuously and his eyes were slitted sceptically.

'You probably didn't want him to stop,' he jibed.

'Yes, I did,' she insisted. 'But he wouldn't listen to me and there was nothing I could do. I couldn't hit him or grab at the steering wheel. There would have been an accident if I had.'

'But there was an accident,' Dugald reminded her softly. 'And why wouldn't you hit him? It sounds most unlike you to draw the line at that. You would have hit me, and you have often enough.'

'Well, you're different,' Elizabeth argued feebly, and looked down quickly so that he wouldn't see the tears of weakness in her eyes. She didn't want to argue with him. She just wanted to be held by him, to be comforted and soothed by his hands and his voice whispering words of love.

'You can say that again,' he remarked sardonically. 'I don't go around kidnapping other guys' wives, for a start. *And* I don't imagine I'm a knight in shining armour rescuing my lady from a fate worse than death, such as sleeping with her husband, and end up nearly killing myself and damaging her!'

'The accident was my fault,' she whispered, still not looking at him.

'How come?'

'I didn't notice when we reached the Castle Douglas road and I didn't tell him to turn left. He went across and up a farm road.'

'Can't he read?' he asked jeeringly.

'Yes, of course he can.'

'Then why didn't he read the sign at the end of the bypass?'

'I don't know. I suppose he didn't see it. You know how dark and drizzly it was last night, and not knowing the area he wouldn't be looking for it.'

Dugald let out one crisp searing oath and her head jerked up as she gave him a startled glance. The curl of his upper lip was even more pronounced, his glance even more contemptuous.

'He must be nuts,' he said scathingly. 'Or he's still on leading reins needing his mother all the time to tell him what to do and which way to go. How old is he?'

'Twenty-four. The same age as I am.'

'I suppose that's why you like him,' he jeered. 'That endearing boyish charm appeals to your maternal instincts. You can order him about and tell him what to do. With him you can be the leader, the boss. He's easy to tame.'

'Oh, I wish you would keep your voice down!' Elizabeth raged, keeping her own voice low. 'Everyone can hear what you're saying and is looking at you. And you ought to watch your language. You might get thrown out of here if you swear again.'

He gave her a mocking glance, then turned round to look at the other people in the room, meeting their surprised and critical stares with a cool confidence, and as soon as they realised he was returning their stares they all began to talk again, averting their glances from him. Slowly he turned back to look at Elizabeth, his eyes glinting with devilry.

'Embarrassed?' he guessed accurately, his glance assessing her.

'By you? Always,' she retorted.

'Then I'll take myself off,' he drawled, and heaved to his feet.

No, don't go! The words screamed through her

mind, but she didn't say them. Instead she sat in straight-backed silence staring down at the bed-clothes, her eyes full of tears.

'I guess Fawley is in love with you, so we can't expect him to behave sensibly,' Dugald said dryly, and looking sideways from beneath her lowered eyelids Elizabeth saw he was still standing beside the bed, his hands in the front pockets of his jeans. All she had to do to touch him was to reach out and pull a hand from a pocket, but she didn't move, she was so afraid of rejection. 'Does he want to marry you?' he asked.

'Yes, he does,' she muttered.

'Then I'll go and look in on him, give him a warning,' he drawled.

'A warning?' she repeated, looking up at him sharply. His face was impassive, the light eyes veiled by their dark lashes. 'What about?' she whispered.

'About you. What else?' he mocked, his eyelids flicking up, his eyes glinting derisively. 'See you tomorrow, maybe,' he added, and turning on his heel he walked away towards the door.

If Elizabeth had been alone she would have flung herself down, pounded the pillows with her fists and wept her heart out. As it was all she could do, aware that some of the visitors were glancing curiously at her, was clench her hands and bite her lip in frustration because the meeting with Dugald had not gone the way she had hoped. The dramatic and sudden ending in an accident to her runaway escapade with Alan had not resulted in Dugald rushing to her side to confess his love for her as she had hoped it would. That sort of thing only happened in novels, she supposed miserably. It didn't happen in real life, or in marriages which had been arranged like hers and Dugald's. The accident hadn't changed anything. All it had done was make her realise how much she was still attracted to Dugald and how much she needed him. She pressed a clenched hand against her lips and bit hard on a knuckle as tears brimmed again and spilled over on to her cheeks. Oh, God, what was she going to do now?

'What's this? Weeping because your visitor has left?' A nurse was beside the bed, thermometer in hand. The instrument slipped into Elizabeth's mouth and her wrist was held between cool fingers while the nurse looked at a watch and counted.

As soon as the thermometer was removed from her mouth Elizabeth asked:

'Will I be able to go home tomorrow?'

'Not if your temperature is up like it is now, nor if your blood pressure is still up,' replied the nurse. 'The best thing for you to do is rest, Mrs Morin, and not get over-excited. I told your husband to phone the ward in the morning about eleven o'clock. We'll tell him then whether he should come and collect you.'

'I'd like to know how Mr Fawley is. Could you find out for me, please?'

'I will. Now, just you lie down and close your eyes, and for goodness' sake stop fretting!'

Elizabeth tried to do as she had been told, but the drowsiness which had claimed her all morning and since lunchtime had gone, put to flight by Dugald's upsetting visit. It was he who excited her always, causing her pulse to race and her nerves to tighten. He had always done that to her. Why? Because she wasn't sure of him. Because she never knew what he was going to do or say next. They had never been able to live in harmony all the time. Always they were pulling in different directions. And yet when passion flared between them and its heat fused their minds and bodies together their union was, or at least had been, always so complete and satisfying, as if they had been created for each other.

Where was he now? Had he gone to see Alan as he had said he would, to warn him? About her, he had said. Probably against her. Probably he would tell Alan that she hadn't been a good wife. And when he left the hospital where would he go? To see Fiona, perhaps. With herself in hospital he was free to spend all his time with his old flame if he wanted. He could stay the night with her or have Fiona stay the night with him at Nethercraig. Oh, God, she couldn't bear the thought of them being together! Jealousy was sweeping over her in a green tide that drowned all her better thoughts and instincts.

The afternoon drifted into evening. The nurse came and told her that Alan was as well as could be expected and that his father had been to see him. A meal was served and she ate a little of it. The night staff came on and patients were prepared for sleep. She swallowed a sleeping pill gratefully, knowing now that it would knock her out and blot all nerve-racking thoughts from her mind. The night passed quickly and she was awakened early. Feeling much more rested, knowing that her pulse rate was normal and her temperature was down, she did nothing to excite herself, determined to leave hospital that day. She was allowed to leave the bed to visit the bathroom and to wash herself, and ate her breakfast sitting in a chair instead of in bed. After her temperature and blood pressure had been checked she was told she could leave hospital as soon as she liked.

'Has my husband phoned?' she asked.

'Yes, and someone is coming to pick you up and take you home,' said the ward Sister. 'You can get dressed if you like and sit in the lounge to wait.'

'Do you think I could go and see my friend Mr Fawley while I'm waiting? I'd like to say goodbye to him.'

'Of course you can. He's in ward six. When you're dressed I'll get one of the student nurses to show you the way.'

Fortunately her clothing had not been damaged in the accident and she looked quite respectable when she was dressed, although very pale. In ward six Alan was, surprisingly, out of his bed which was being re-made and he was sitting in a wheelchair with his right leg, which was in a cast, stuck out straight before him. He looked pale too and as soon as he saw her he stretched out his hands to her and she took them in both of hers.

'I'm so sorry,' she said. 'It's all my fault that you're hurt. I should have been watching. If I'd been looking I'd have directed you on to the right road as soon as we reached the bypass.'

'No, no,' he argued urgently, 'you mustn't say that. It wasn't your fault, it was mine. I should have listened to you and not tried to make you run away with me. I should have taken you to the hotel for dinner and behaved in a civilised way.' He rumpled his fair hair with one hand and his wide boyish smile appeared. 'The trouble was, I was angry and jealous. I couldn't bear to think of you having to ... to live with ... that ... that man. To think of you having to put up with his ... his ...' he broke off, his face twisting with the agony of his thoughts, 'with his hands touching you,' he added in a whisper. 'And I went a little out of my mind. I couldn't think straight or act sensibly. All I could do was take you away from him. I still want to take you away from him.'

'Please, Alan, calm down. There's no need for you to get so excited,' said Elizabeth. 'I just came in to say goodbye. I'll be going to Nethercraig in a few minutes. I believe your father came to see you yesterday.'

'He arrived in the evening. He's taking me back to Brancaster this afternoon.' He looked up at her pleadingly, still clinging to one of her hands. 'Come with us, Elizabeth.'

'I ... I ... can't. I have an appointment with the solicitor in Duncraig tomorrow. Will you have to go into Brancaster hospital?'

'No, as long as I don't do anything too energetic for a while they think I'll be okay. I'll be able to get about on crutches,' he replied, adding with a change of tone, 'Morin came to see me yesterday afternoon after he'd been to see you.'

'I hope he wasn't rude to you.'

'No, not really. He said you had told him that I

want to marry you and thought he ought to warn me that we would have to wait a while before that could happen.'

'What did he mean?' she exclaimed.

'I don't know, but I got the impression that if you were to ask him now he'll agree to a divorce some time later this year.' He smiled again suddenly and winked at her. 'Even if we didn't have a night away together we seem to have got our point across to him, don't we? He's aware now that you don't want to stay married to him.'

'All right, Mr Fawley, I'm going to take you to be fitted for some crutches,' said a male nurse, coming up and taking hold of the back of the wheelchair. 'Excuse us, miss.'

'Goodbye, Alan,' Elizabeth said.

'Come back to Brancaster soon,' he replied as he was pushed towards the ward doors.

Elizabeth found her way back to the lounge of the other ward, and had to admit she was quite glad to sit down. It was quarter to twelve. Dugald would be there in about ten minutes. She leaned back and closed her eyes, thinking over the recent conversation with Alan. Dugald had talked to him much more directly than he ever talked to her and had indicated that he wouldn't oppose a divorce. But how could he inherit anything from Hunter if he agreed to a divorce? Had he changed his mind and decided that he didn't want to stay married to her after all, not even to benefit from Hunter's will? She would have to ask him as soon as she saw him. They had to discuss their situation quietly and sensibly before tomorrow.

Footsteps were coming along the corridor;

female footsteps, judging by the click of high heels on the vinyl floor covering. They stopped outside the partially open door of the lounge. Knuckles rapped on the door and it was pushed open. Fiona, wearing a powder-blue woollen suit with a pleated skirt and a blazer-styled jacket, walked in.

'Oh, my dear Liza, how ghastly you look!' she exclaimed, while Elizabeth stared at her. 'How do you feel? Are you sure you're well enough to leave hospital? Perhaps you should have another day's rest.'

'I'm all right,' Elizabeth replied, rising to her feet. 'Just surprised, that's all, to see you here. Where's Dugald?'

'He wanted to go to the island, to Mindoon, while the tide was out this morning, and it was low at tide at eleven-thirty. It meant that he'd be later coming for you, so I offered to come for you instead while he went to look at the cottage. We knew you would understand. You do, don't you?'

'I . . . er . . . yes, I suppose I do,' muttered Elizabeth. Disappointment was like a kick in the ribs, leaving a pain around her heart.

'He wanted to have a look at the cottage before that interview with Mr Bothwell tomorrow, so he can say everything is in good order there or not, as the case may be,' said Fiona. 'Here, take my arm and lean on me just as much as you like. I'm sure you must be feeling awfully weak.'

'No, I'm not,' snapped Elizabeth. 'And I don't need your arm to lean on.'

'Oh, all right, as you wish,' replied Fiona in her placid way. 'I thought we'd have a chance to talk on the drive back to Kilford. It's such a long time since you and I had a heart-to-heart, isn't it?'

Outside the sun was as warm as if it were June and not April and in the garden in front of the hospital tulips, crimson orange and gold, stood soldier-straight in the borders. In the town the old granite buildings sparkled in the sunlight. It was a good day on which to be alive, thought Elizabeth, and wished suddenly she could be with Dugald walking around the island where they had first made love together, perhaps forgetting the time and letting the tide cover the ridge of sand and shingle, to spend the afternoon and night in the cottage, reviving the romance there had once been between them, renewing their commitment to one another.

'I thought we'd go back the pretty way,' said Fiona brightly as they left the town behind and she turned the car down a narrow lane which wound past green fields where lambs frisked. 'It's such a lovely day and the coastline between Glencairn and Binary Bay is very attractive; I always think.'

In a few minutes the Firth came into sight, its smooth water shimmering with silvery light, small islands, blobs of yellow, pink and green, seeming to float on it. Fiona turned the car to the right and followed the narrow dusty road which twisted up and down hill, past farmhouses and fields on one side and the rocky scattered sandy beaches on the other. Across a wide bay, in the far distance, the houses of Kilford twinkled small glints of white against the hunched green shoulder of Upper Craig Hill.

'Why didn't you and Alan go to the hotel last night for dinner, as we'd arranged?' Fiona asked in her pleasant diplomatic way, as if nothing unusual had occurred the night before.

'Alan decided he didn't want to have dinner there,' replied Elizabeth stiffly. Not for anything was she going to admit to Fiona that she had almost run away with Alan.

'Dugald and I were quite worried when you weren't there, but we thought you would turn up sooner or later, so we sat down to dinner. It was very good too. I had venison pie. Mrs Arnott is really an extremely good cook. I enjoyed it, but I could see Dugald was anxious when you hadn't arrived by the time we'd finished. He thought you might have had an accident somewhere, so after he'd taken me home he went to look for you. He said he didn't trust Alan . . . as a driver, I assumed he meant,' Fiona flicked a sideways glance at Elizabeth. 'He even went so far as to say he wished I hadn't shown Alan the way to Nethercraig. He said you and he were just getting somewhere, beginning to agree about something, when I rang the doorbell.' Again the sideways flick of very blue eyes. 'Were you?'

'Yes, I suppose we were,' Elizabeth muttered, gazing out at the sea. It was azure blue now, reflecting the sky, and was flecked by silver ripples, and she could just see the mountains on the other shore, a smudge of violet haze.

'About a divorce, perhaps?' Fiona probed.

'Why should we discuss divorce?' countered Elizabeth cautiously.

'Well, you have been separated for two and a

half years. Another six months and you could get one very easily. I'd supposed that was what you were both intending to do.'

'Did Dugald tell you that?'

'Not exactly. But he did say something last night about Mr Finley's will putting both of you in a difficult position.' Fiona changed gear to take the steep incline which curved away from the sea inland to pass between thick hedges of rhododendron and laurel bushes which screened some isolated cottages from the road. 'I must say I wouldn't have thought Mr Finley could be so cruel as to impose conditions on you. He must have known that you and Dugald had found out you couldn't live together. It's always been obvious ... to me, at any rate ... that you and Dugald are incompatible.'

Elizabeth was silent, watching the shadows of trees flick past the car, sifting through what Fiona had said, trying to find the message she was sure Fiona was attempting to convey to her. After a while she said,

'You're in love with Dugald, aren't you? I should have guessed that you were before this, but I didn't until last night when I saw the way you looked at him when he came into the sitting room. You and Dugald were having an affair when Hunter suggested Dugald should ask me to marry him, weren't you?'

'No, not an affair. Not in the accepted sense of the word,' replied Fiona, shaking her head. 'But I think he would have asked me to marry him that summer, three years ago, if he hadn't met you and if Mr Finley hadn't urged him ... perhaps I should say *bribed* him to marry you,' she added sneeringly. 'I thought I would get over it. I thought I would forget him, but two and a half years ago when he came to Kilford too late for your first anniversary and I met him again I knew that it wasn't over for either of us. I think he did too, but he was reluctant to break with you until I told him what you had told me.'

'What had I told you?' exclaimed Elizabeth.

'That you'd married him for the same reason he'd married you—because Mr Finley had pressured you into marriage so that you would benefit from his will.'

'But I only said that. . . .' Elizabeth began, and broke off to look away through the window again. The road was slanting down to the estuary and she could see the bridge which spanned the marshes and the channel of the river not far from the old ford which gave Kilford its name. The houses which had been glints of white at a distance were distinct shapes now, squares, rectangles and triangles gleaming in the sunlight against the dark greens of the hill. The tide was coming in slowly and the river was swelling and spreading over the brown banks of mud in a shimmering greenish-grey wave, and the small boats which had been lying on their sides were beginning to tilt upright and to float.

For a moment she relived again that time in the sitting room at Nethercraig when she had been so upset by what Fiona had told her about Dugald and her pride had dictated that she should pretend to be unconcerned by pointing out that she had known all along about the arrangement for her marriage to Dugald. Her hands clenched on her knees as she felt a wild urge to hit Fiona and accuse her of being a telltale. Fiona had told Dugald what she had said. No wonder he had been so hostile towards her when she had said she had wanted to stay in Britain and take another degree! No wonder he had accused her of marrying him only to please Hunter and her mother.

Fiona had primed them both, telling each of them tales about the other so that they had distrusted each other. And they had listened to her and had believed her instead of listening to and believing each other. Why? Because both of them had known Fiona longer than they had known each other.

'You must have been pleased when you heard that Dugald and I had separated,' she said coldly, as the car passed over the stone bridge and turned on to the road which went through the village.

'Oh, not pleased. One can never be pleased when one hears of the break-up of a marriage of two dear friends,' replied Fiona sadly. 'But I wasn't surprised. The break-up was on the cards from the very beginning of the game. You and Dugald are so unsuited to each other.'

'What makes you think that?'

'You have such different backgrounds, so you have different attitudes to life. He's such a traditionalist in outlook, really. He believes a woman's place is in the home, having children, caring for her husband and making him comfortable, and you're very liberated and career-orientated. You were bound to clash and quarrel. I'm surprised Mr Finley didn't notice your incompatibility.'

What had Hunter seen that summer? Elizabeth wondered as the car crawled up the hill past Castle Craig Hotel. Cars were coming the other way, indicating that the Sunday morning church service was over. She had intended to go to church this morning since it was the first Sunday after Hunter's death. He would have liked her and Dugald to have been at the service to pray for him.

She tried to put herself in his place three years ago when she and Dugald had met. He must have seen how wary they had been of each other at first. Had he said something to Dugald and was that why Dugald had made the first advance? After that Hunter must have seen two passionate lovers incapable of staying apart from one another for very long. He must have seen two high-spirited, independent persons coming together, two equals arguing, battling, playing, laughing and loving together, and he must have been delighted that his plan for their union had worked out.

'Dugald and I have had so little time together, really,' she explained. 'We've never had much chance to get to know one another well. I suppose you're hoping we'll divorce so you can marry him?'

Fiona slowed the car as they approached the entrance to Nethercraig's driveway and turned the car between the gateposts before answering.

'I think I can be honest with you,' she said. 'Yes, I do hope you'll get a divorce, and I said as much to Dugald last night at dinner.'

'What did he say?' asked Elizabeth in a small,

miserable voice as Fiona brought the car to a stop in front of the house.

Fiona put the brake on and turned off the ignition before she replied. Then she turned to look at Elizabeth, the expression in her blue eyes rather pitying.

'He warned me that it will be some time before he can ask you for a divorce. He says he wants to make quite sure the terms of Mr Finley's will are carried out, and to do that he has to stay married to you for a while.' Fiona sighed and her glance swerved away from Elizabeth's wide, troubled gaze. 'Two to three years, he said, before anything can be done and . . . well, anything could happen in that time. You and he could have children.' The cool voice shook a little and broke. 'Oh, Elizabeth,' Fiona whispered. 'Can't you persuade him not to stay married to you? He says he's only going through with it for your sake and Mr Finley's sake.'

'For my sake? What do you mean?' exclaimed Elizabeth.

'He wants to make sure that you'll inherit Nethercraig and the investments because that's really what Mr Finley wanted. He wanted a Finley to inherit. Then when the terms of the will have been fulfilled Dugald will make arrangements for you to divorce him and he'll make sure that you get his half of everything in the divorce settlement.' Again Fiona's voice shook and she looked away quickly. 'But it will take so long,' she sighed. 'It will take so long.'

There was silence in the car. Outside birds whistled among the trees and shrubs. Bright daffodils and tulips edging the driveway swayed in the light wind. The granite walls of the house sparkled in the sunlight. There was no small orange car parked in the driveway.

'Dugald's car isn't here,' said Elizabeth dully. 'Did he drive to Mindoon, across the causeway?'

'Yes, I believe he did,' replied Fiona. 'But he must have come back. I know he didn't intend to stay there for very long.'

'Unless he got caught by the tide,' said Elizabeth. 'Then he would have to stay.' She opened the door of the car. 'Thank you for coming to meet me, Fiona. I suppose I won't be seeing you again because you'll be going back to Glasgow to-night.'

'Oh, I have a few hours to spare before I have to leave,' said Fiona. 'Since Dugald isn't here let's go and have some lunch at the hotel. They do quite a good bar lunch on a Sunday and you must be in need of food. I know I am. Shall we go?'

'All right.' Elizabeth closed the door of the car. She didn't want to be with Fiona any longer, but she knew there wasn't much food in the house and she didn't feel like preparing a meal by herself.

Castle Craig Hotel was a square three-storeyed house built on Upper Craig Hill. It was made from blocks of grey granite stone quarried locally and it commanded magnificent views of the estuary and the silvery, island-dotted Firth. There were several cars parked in its courtyard and the small bar was full of people having lunch. Most of the people were from houses in the area and knew both Fiona and Elizabeth, so for a while they were both busy exchanging greetings.

They ordered their lunch at the bar and taking the glasses of sherry they had both chosen they went and sat at a table in the corner to wait to be served. Elizabeth drank some of her sherry quickly. She felt in need of some stimulus. The medium-sweet tawny liquid seeped down her throat, warming her. She watched Fiona sipping daintily, tried to imagine the woman married to Dugald and failed.

'Supposing Dugald and I do get a divorce,' she said quietly, leaning forward so that no one else in the room could possibly hear what she was saying, 'how do you know he'll marry you and not Michèle?'

'Michèle?' queried Fiona, looking up with a frown of puzzlement.

'You know, the woman in Montreal you told me about. He's still friendly with her and pays the rent for her apartment.'

Fiona's beautiful blue eyes went wide with surprise and shock.

'How do you know that?' she whispered.

'I asked him the other day when he arrived here.'

'Are you implying that he's been living with her?' Fiona gasped, a strange expression flitting across her face, a mixture of horror and disgust.

'Your guess is as good as mine,' replied Elizabeth, feeling a little flicker of triumph because for once she was one up on Fiona.

'But that's ... that's horrible, perfectly horrible!' gasped Fiona. 'I mean, it's ... it's incest!'

'Incest?' Elizabeth exclaimed, her eyes widening too. 'Why do you say that?'

'Well, Michèle is Dugald's half-sister. His father was married twice. Didn't you know?'

CHAPTER SIX

THE April twilight was long that evening, the light reluctant to leave the sky once the sun had set or the darkness reluctant to come—Elizabeth couldn't decide which as she walked round the tarn at Nethercraig. Reaching the edge of the lawn where the land fell away to the rocky shore, she stared at the view. The curves of the hills on the opposite shore of the river estuary were deep purple against the pale green sky. Water in the estuary was pewter grey, rippled here and there with violet shadows. Her glance moved on to the small island, a dark mysterious shape now against the pale water, and she wondered if Dugald was still there, staying in the cottage, waiting for the tide to go out so that he could drive back to the mainland across the causeway of mud and shingle.

She turned away to walk back to the house. The barks of silver birches glimmered in the fading light against the background of dark spruces and pines. Nethercraig's windows glinted too like so many eyes in a solid shadowed face, like Dugald's eyes glinted surprisingly light against his olive skin, icy cold. The windows of his soul? Elizabeth smiled a little wryly. The only time his eyes looked warm was when he wanted her, when he lusted after her body.

Reaching the french window of the sitting

room, she looked back once more to the island. Was he really there? Or had he gone somewhere else for the day? All afternoon she had been hoping he would come back. After Fiona had left to drive back to Glasgow she had used the time alone to search for the rest of the items of furniture, antique dishes and pottery, silver and pewter mugs which Hunter had specified in his will to be given to his friends and helpers.

She had found everything and had made a note of their location, and now she was wishing Dugald would come so that they could have a proper and sensible discussion about what they were going to do tomorrow when they went to see Mr Bothwell again. Then she would confront him again with the matter of divorce and insist that he give her a straight answer. She was tired of finding out what he wanted to do from other people. It was time he communicated directly with her, without arguing or quarrelling. If only he would come!

She stepped into the sitting room and closed the french window, then drew the heavy crimson velvet curtains across. Supposing he didn't come? Supposing he had left, walked out because he was so disgusted with the difficult situation Hunter had created? It hadn't occurred to her before that he might leave. Suddenly she was running towards the hall. She hurried up the stairs and into her bedroom. Although she had been up before to change from the dress she had been wearing into slacks and a sweater she hadn't stayed long in the room. Now she looked around it closely. Dugald's cases were still there, placed side by side near the wardrobe, and her breath came out in a ragged sigh of relief. He wouldn't have left without them. Slowly she wandered over to the chest of drawers, noting some papers lying there. His passport was there. Idly she turned over the other papers—envelopes containing letters, official-looking documents, nothing that seemed to be personal. She pulled her hand back sharply, as if she had been burned, and turned away. Once bitten, twice shy. Never again was she going to look through any correspondence belonging to Dugald. She didn't want to find any more letters from women she didn't know, from Michèle. Oh, surely he hadn't lived with her? Surely he wasn't so morally corrupt that he would do something like that.

She opened the passport, though, to look at his photograph. As usual it didn't do justice to the subject. He looked tough and grim, a ruffian with cold hard eyes; eyes which were good at assessing the geological formation of the land. He had done well in his work, so well that he had formed his own company of mining consultants. Hunter had told her that when she had visited him at Christmas.

'Knows what he's doing, does Dugald,' Hunter had said proudly. 'And isn't afraid to take a chance, to gamble on his hunches about what lies in the ground, to buy land where he believes there are natural resources and to profit from their discovery. He'll be a millionaire one of these days, you mark my words. He's not doing badly now and he doesn't really need what I'm going to leave to him . . . *if* you and he stayed married to each other. It's time you were reconciled. I don't hold with this separation and divorce business, you know.'

Dugald didn't need the money because he was already wealthy. He didn't need Nethercraig either because he wasn't going to make his home here, if he was successful in Canada. He didn't need Elizabeth if he could have Fiona who would do all the right things, would make a home for him, have his children and raise them, make him comfortable, do everything a good wife should.

But she was also capable of doing all those things for him now, Elizabeth thought as she wandered down the stairs again and into Hunter's favourite room, a sort of study-lounge behind the sun-porch, a comfortable room where there were no antiques, and where it was possible to be lazy, even to sleep. She switched on the desk lamp, drew the curtains and looked round. In a glass-fronted cabinet Hunter's small supply of bottles of liquor and wine glinted, with some glasses. Going over to it, she opened it and found a bottle of sherry. She poured some into a glass and went to sit down in one of the armchairs.

Yes, she could do all the things a wife could do, all the things Dugald had once accused her of being incapable of doing. She just need a little encouragement ... from him. She needed to be told that he loved her and needed her. If he told her she was more important to him than any other person in the world, if he worshipped her a little, like Alan did. . . .

She got to her feet restlessly, empty glass in hand, and went back to the cabinet to pour more sherry. She didn't want to marry Alan and she didn't want a divorce so she could marry him. She wanted to be married to Dugald. She *was* married to Dugald, so why even consider discussing divorce with him? Why not go to the solicitor's office tomorrow and swear that she was going to remain married to him? Why not go to bed with him and conceive his child so that he would have to stay married to her . . . at least until the child was born?

She drank all the sherry in the glass and set it down. It made her feel warm inside. Now if only Dugald would come she would show him how much she wanted him. Leaving the room, she went upstairs again and into the bathroom to turn on the bathtaps. For the next half hour she luxuriated in soft water foaming with scented bubbles. When she was dry she dressed in a long nightgown, made from peach pink satin and lace. Long-sleeved with a high round neck, it was demure and had little bows of ribbon to fasten the long slit opening at the front. Her white skin gleamed invitingly through the lacy panels.

Standing in front of the dressing-table mirror, she brushed her hair, lifting the brush through it from underneath so that it thickened and frizzed about her face like a halo, glowing with sunset lights. When she was satisfied that she looked seductive she went downstairs to the study again and picking up the bottle of sherry and her empty glass went through to the sitting room.

Jane had left some logs on the cast-iron dog grate for a fire and they were soon crackling as flames leapt about them. Elizabeth lit the candles in the handsome silver candlesticks on the mantelpiece and then the candles in the matching candelabrum on the grand piano. Switching off the electric lights, she curled up in a corner of the long chesterfield by the fire and sipped more sherry. The firelight and the candlelight glinted on silver and polished wood. The shadows were deep and romantic. All that was lacking was the sweet soft music, she thought with a whimsical little smile, and the scene was set for seduction.

The warmth from the fire and the sherry both had their effect on her, tired as she was from the aftermath of the accident and anxiety about the situation between herself and Dugald. With her head resting against a plump soft cushion, she slipped into sleep. An hour later she awakened with a start, roused by the sound of something falling. The sherry glass had fallen from her lax hand to the floor. Feeling cold, she looked round the shadowed room. The fire had died down to a few ashes and glowing embers. The candles were guttering, long drips of wax winding round them.

Her head heavy, her neck cricked, she stood up, blew out the candles and groped her way from the room into the hall. Dugald hadn't come. Perhaps he would never come. She might as well go to bed. Slowly she went up the stairs, holding on to the banisters. She felt very groggy. She must have drunk too much sherry, or she had overdone things instead of resting as she had been advised by the doctor at the hospital. In the bedroom she pushed back the bedclothes and climbed into bed. She was just drifting off to sleep again when another sound, like a door being banged, shut brought her upright, her eyes wide, her nerves crawling with tension.

Her heart racing madly, she listened. A wind had got up and the trees outside the bedroom window were creaking. Perhaps she had left an outside door open and the wind had blown it shut and that was the noise she had heard. It would be best if she checked. Pushing aside the bedclothes, she swung off the bed, her feet groping for her slippers and finding them. Opening the bedroom door, she put her head out and listened again. Only the wind in the trees, and yet she had a gut feeling that someone was in the house.

Quietly she crept out on to the dark landing to the head of the stairs and looked over the banisters into the well of the hall. Its darkness was splintered with faint yellow light. Had she left a light on downstairs after all? She couldn't remember whether she had switched off the light in the study. While she hesitated she heard another sound, the unmistakable tinkle of breaking glass.

Down the stairs she plunged, finding the steps instinctively, running her hand along the banisters to guide herself. In the hallway she paused to catch her breath. Light was slanting out from the study. She crept towards it and peered through the opening where the door was hinged to the jamb. The reading lamp on the desk was on. Its light glinted on the bottle which was being set down by a large hand; a man's hand. His back was to the door and his clothes were unrecognisable because he was behind the light, silhouetted against it. On the desk were two glasses, one half full of liquor, the other broken.

Turning suddenly before she lost courage, Elizabeth pushed open the door and marched into the room. The man swung round to face her. Light eyes flashed in surprise in a dark, hawkish face.

'Liz!' Dugald exclaimed. 'What are you doing here? I thought you'd gone to Brancaster.'

'Brancaster?' she repeated foolishly, staring at him. His dark hair was spiky, sticking out all over the place as if he had been out in a high wind, his face was pale and taut and his eyes were red-rimmed as if he had driven a long way in the dark. He picked up the glass containing whisky and drank half the liquor before answering her.

'That's right,' he said. 'You weren't at the hospital when I arrived there and the ward Sister didn't know where you were. She said you'd gone to visit Fawley, so I went along to his ward.' He raised the glass and finished the remains of the whisky, turning to pour more from the bottle. 'I was told that he'd gone back to Brancaster,' he said in a flat cold voice. 'I assumed you'd gone with him.'

'But—but ... oh, I don't understand,' she complained, a hand pressed against her forehead. 'Fiona said you'd gone over to Mindoon to look at the cottage and make sure it was all right, so she offered to go to the hospital for me and you agreed to let her go.'

Dugald picked up his refilled glass and slanted her a narrowed glance.

'She did, eh?' he drawled, his mouth twisting at one corner. 'I did go over to the island, but I was going to come back before the tide turn and drive straight to the hospital for you. And that's exactly what I did.'

'Did you tell Fiona that was what you were going to do?'

'Of course I did,' he snapped. 'She called in here just as I was leaving for the island. She was on her way to church, she said, and wanted to know what had happened to you. She must have taken it into her own head to go and fetch you. She might have left a note!' His voice rasped with irritation. 'It would have saved me a lot of trouble if she had. But why didn't I pass you on the road?'

'We . . . we came back the pretty way,' she explained, watching him toss back the contents of the glass, realising how neatly Fiona had tricked both of them. 'I've been here all afternoon and evening. I thought perhaps you'd been trapped by the tide coming in on the island and would come back as soon as it was out at midnight. It must be about midnight now. Where have you been all this time?'

'Been worried?' His right eyebrow flicked upwards sardonically.

'No, not particularly,' she replied evasively. 'But it's time we met to discuss what we're going to do tomorrow.'

Glass in his hand, he flopped back into Hunter's old leather-covered swivel chair. He drank more whisky, lowered the glass and gave her another underbrowed glance.

'I went to see Jan Dobie. He and I were students together,' he replied slowly. 'He lives near Glasgow and is married now and has a couple of kids. We talked, had a few drinks, I stayed for dinner.' He shrugged, finished the whisky and set the glass down. 'What have you been doing?' he asked.

'I've found all the pictures, pieces of furniture and other bequests mentioned in Hunter's will. I've made a list of them and written their location and the names and addresses of the people who are to receive them beside each item. The list is on the desk, there.' Going round the desk to stand beside him, Elizabeth pointed to the neatly typed list. Dugald picked it up and studied it.

'Mmm, knowing how to make catalogues in a library comes in useful sometimes,' he mocked. 'I hadn't realised you could be so efficient.'

'There's a lot you don't know about me,' she retorted. He tossed the list back on to the desk and his glance moved slowly upwards, lingering on the line of her thigh showing beneath the silky satin of the nightgown, before moving on up over her flat stomach to the curves and uptilted points of her breasts peeping coyly through the panel of peach-coloured lace. His eyelashes flicked up suddenly and his eyes met hers. No longer ice-cold, they blazed with naked desire, and she felt her body grow taut with answering desire almost as if he had touched and inflamed tender, vulnerable nerves.

'I know what matters,' he said softly.

'But not enough,' she replied, and half sat on the desk. 'We must discuss what we're going to do.'

'Must we? I thought we knew what we have to do. Tomorrow we're going to Bothwell's office to say we'll stay married and then we'll inherit this house and the investments, and we'll live happily ever after.' Irony rasped in the depths of his voice and his mouth twisted cynically as he reached out a hand for the bottle of whisky to tilt it over his glass.

'But you said we'd talk about it privately first,' Elizabeth protested.

'I know I did.' He picked up the glass and surveyed her. 'I had to say that to stop you from throwing everything away without consideration. If I hadn't stopped you, you would have denied Hunter his lifelong wish, which was to make sure a Finley ... that is, you ... received this house and his money so that they could be passed on to your descendants.'

'I still think we should talk it out,' she argued. 'We haven't come to an agreement yet.'

Dugald sipped more whisky, considering her shape again. He set the almost empty glass down and leaned towards her, his lips curving in a slight, taunting smile which seemed to threaten her.

'We were pretty close to an agreement on Friday night, when we were in bed,' he said.

'Oh, that's all you ever think about!' she flared.

'Only when you're around, sweetheart,' he retorted, sliding a hand along the line of her thigh where it rested on the desk, his touch gentle yet provocative as he watched her with brilliant, dark-lashed eyes. 'In fact, I think we should go to bed right now and do our talking there,' he suggested.

'No!' She slid off the desk and went round to the other side so that it was a barrier between him and her. 'Not until we've had everything out in the open.'

'What the hell do you mean by everything?' he growled irritably, lunging to his feet and walking round the desk towards her.

'I mean that I want to know just what it is you have in mind to do after ... after ... we've inherited Hunter's property,' she replied, her head up. 'Are you going to stay here or are you going back to Canada?'

He pulled up short and folding his arms glowered at her, his black eyebrows forming a straight bar above the high bridge of his nose, his glance hard and cold again, his lips set in a tight line.

'I'll be going back to Canada. My business is there,' he rasped.

'To live with Michèle?' She forced the words out.

'To what?' he exclaimed, his eyebrows lifting in surprise.

'Are you going to live with Michèle again, play house with her in Montreal?' she said jibingly.

'Why the hell would I want to live with her?' he asked slowly, obviously bewildered by the question.

'You pay the rent for the apartment where she lives, so I assume you'll want to share it with her.'

'I do not pay the rent for an apartment for her,' he retorted, frowning at her again. 'She doesn't live in an apartment. She and Jules live in a very pleasant split-level house in one of the suburbs.'

'But you said you still pay the rent on that apartment she said she'd decorated in the letter I found,' she accused.

'Where did you find the letter?' he asked quietly.

'In the waste paper basket in my bedroom at the flat in Brancaster. It was with another letter which had been written to you while you were in South America.'

'So you didn't find it until I'd left!' Dugald exclaimed.

'No, I didn't.'

'Then why did you say on Friday that knowing about Michèle was one of your reasons for wanting a separation if you didn't know about her until after I'd left Brancaster?'

'But I did know about her before I found the letter,' she said, backing away from him as he began to walk towards her again.

'Who told you about her?'

'Fiona did,' she whispered, grabbing a small chair and putting it between them, effectively stopping him.

'Michèle is my half-sister,' he said abruptly, picking up the chair and placing it to one side, then coming towards her again.

'I know that now. Fiona told me today, and I think it's disgusting that you've lived with Michèle and you keep her as if she's your mistress,' she blurted, stepping back and colliding with the door, inadvertently closing it.

Again Dugald stopped. He stared at her incredulously for a moment, then tipping back his head he burst out laughing.

'My God, you've really been raking around in the mud, haven't you?' he jeered, 'trying to find reasons why you shouldn't have anything to do with me. You'll be accusing me of murder next!' He stepped right up to her and thrust his face close to hers. 'Listen carefully to what I have to say, sweetheart, because it's the truth and you'd better believe it. Michèle does not live in an apartment for which I pay rent, nor is she my mistress. She lives with her husband Jules and their three daughters. She's very happily married to Jules. The apartment I pay rent for is mine. Michèle found it for me while I was working in South America. She happens to to be an expert on interior decoration and furniture design, so at my request she had the apartment decorated and furnished so that it would be ready when I returned from South America and so that I had somewhere to offer you as a home.' He drew back and turning away went back to the desk to pick up the whisky bottle. 'God, what does it matter now? You killed that dream for me when you said you wanted to stay in Brancaster to work, when you said you didn't want to be a full-time wife or a mother,' he added savagely, and sloshed whisky into his glass. Picking the glass up, he tossed down most of the liquor, then turned to face her, his eyes glittering with hostility.

'If ... if ... I'd known I wouldn't have,' Elizabeth began miserably, then flung her head back and glared at him. 'It was your own fault!' she flared. 'You ... you never told me anything about yourself. Why didn't you tell me you had a half-sister?'

'I don't know,' he shrugged, studying the glints of light on the facets of the cut glass tumbler in his hand. 'I suppose I assumed you knew about her, that Hunter or my mother had told you.' He looked across at her, his eyes opaque, smoky grey under heavy lids. 'Relatives, family history— things like that weren't important at the time,' he murmured, and put the glass down on the desk. He walked over to her again. 'All that mattered was what happened when you and I were to- gether,' he murmured, raising a hand to touch her hair. 'It's happening now,' he added in a suggest- ive whisper, stroking the hair back from her ear, from her throat, his fingers gentle yet titillating as they slid round to the nape of her neck.

'We've never communicated properly, never,' she muttered, her glance going to his mouth.

'Yes, we have, in the best possible way.'

As the fingers at her neck impelled her forward his other hand slid over her hip round to the small of her back and her whole body quivered in re- sponse. She swayed towards him, her face lifting to his, her lips parting in mute invitation to be kissed.

'You see?' he said, his breath warm and moist against her lips, giving her a foretaste of what his kiss would be like. 'We're communicating now.'

The smell of whisky was tangy-sweet in her nostrils, rising drug-like to her brain.

'You've been drinking a lot,' she rebuked him, putting her arms round his neck and ruffling the hair at his nape.

Dugald sniffed and then rubbed his nose against hers in a delightfully primitive and simple caress.

'You've had a few yourself, my tiger lady,' he

whispered mockingly. Then his arms tightened convulsively about her and his lips moved in sensual persuasion against the curve of her neck. 'Let's go to bed, Liza,' he whispered.

Every nerve in her body quivered in response to that appeal, but she was still distrustful of his motives in wanting to make love to her. With her hands against his shoulders she pushed him away slightly, her eyes searching his face. Desire had lit flames in his eyes and even though she had pushed him away his hands still moved seductively up her back.

'For all I know you might only want to get me into bed to make me pregnant so that the terms of Hunter's will can be fulfilled,' she challenged him.

'And for all I know you might be responding to me because you want to get pregnant,' he retorted softly, the corner of his mouth quirking upwards in that slight smile that always seemed to mock her.

'I wish I knew why. I wish you'd tell me why,' she complained.

'I don't know why,' he evaded, drawing her against his hard body. 'I only know you turn me on, Liza, and that's enough reason for me.' Reaching behind her, he turned the doorknob and pulled the door open, then with a quick movement he swung her up in his arms and carried her into the hallway.

'Why aren't you fighting, tiger lady?' he asked mockingly as he carried her up the stairs. 'Why aren't you clawing at me with your nails, hitting me with your fists?'

'Because fighting you won't stop you, it never

has,' she replied dreamily, lifting her arms about his neck again and leaning her head against his shoulder, glorying for the first time in his superior strength.

'It seems you have learned something about me since we've been married, after all,' he taunted.

In the moon-dappled darkness of the bedroom he laid her on the bed and lying down beside her gathered her into his arms. A new gentleness in his touch, a lingering reverence in his caresses soon aroused her desire to fever pitch and she was the one who became demanding, her nails scratching his skin as she tugged at his shirt opening to lay bare his chest, her teeth nipping sharply at the hard smoothness of his muscular shoulders.

Yet still it was important to make it clear to him why she was there. She didn't want him to think it was for some ulterior motive.

'I'm not doing this to trap you,' she whispered. 'I'm not doing it to make you stay married to me if you don't want to stay married to me. It doesn't commit either of us to anything.'

'Then why are you doing it?' he asked, pushing her back against the pillows and leaning over her so he could undo the tiny bows which fastened her nightgown, pulling at the ribbons slowly and tantalisingly.

'Because I can't help it,' she admitted sighingly, her body arching up against his when at last his hand cupped her breast. 'And because I like it,' she groaned in an agony of pleasure. 'Oh, please, please,' she gasped. 'I want you, I want you!'

With a soft triumphant laugh Dugald moved against her, his mouth covering hers, and after that passion erupted like a volcano, smothering them with a fierce heat, fusing their bodies together more than once until at last, satiated, they lay curled together in intimate, healing slumber.

When Elizabeth woke up she was alone and the room was full of soft spring sunshine. She lay for a while blinking sleepily, listening to the birds singing and slowly becoming aware of a difference in herself. There was an ease in her body and mind she had never known before. She felt complete, and she wished she could feel like that always, like a musical instrument which has been tuned perfectly.

Pushing up on an elbow, she looked round the room. Dugald's suitcases were still there by the wardrobe and the clothes which he had been wearing the previous day, and which she had removed from him with her own hands, lay scattered about the floor where she had tossed them. The bedroom door was wide open and she could hear water gurgling through pipes as the bath was filled. From the bathroom came the deep rumble of Dugald's voice as he sang to himself.

Jumping out of bed, Elizabeth found her dressing gown, wrapped it around her and tied the belt. In slippered feet she padded along the landing and stopped outside the bathroom. On a sudden impulse she turned the doorknob and pushed. The door was unlocked and opened easily. Looking into the steam-filled room she saw Dugald, his skin shining with moisture, standing beside the bath. He was holding her bottle of foaming bath oil in one hand and seemed intent on pouring most of the contents into the water.

'Oh, that's far too much!' she cried, going into the room and reaching out to take the bottle from him. He let her have it easily and she put it down on the shelf above the wash-hand basin.

'Have you come to join me?' he asked as he turned off the taps and bent over the bath to swish the water. Masses of tiny bubbles foamed immediately, rising until they were above the edge of the bath.

'No, thanks,' she replied. 'I just looked in to ask if it's coffee or tea for you.'

'Coffee. Can you make it?'

'Of course I can.'

'Come and bath first,' he invited, stepping close to her, his hands going to the knot in the tie-belt of her robe and loosening it.

'No. No!' She tried to pull the belt out of his hand and somehow the robe came off her and was snatched away and tossed into a corner. Big hands curved about her slender waist and she was lifted from the floor. 'No, no, Dugald!' she shouted, hitting down at his head and his shoulders with her fists. 'The water will spill over and make such a mess. No, don't tip me in . . . aah!'

Almost an hour later, her hair a wet tangle, her body still tingling from his caresses, her skin glowing from the towelling he had given it, she went downstairs, smiling to herself, the mysterious smile of a woman who has got what she wanted. The grandfather clock in the hall chimed the half hour. Half-past eleven and they hadn't breakfasted yet. In two and a half hours they would be arriving at Mr Bothwell's office and she was still not sure what she was going to do, whether she was going to swear she would stay married to Dugald or not. Oh, she knew she wanted to stay married to him, but she didn't want him to think she would be staying married to him just because she wanted to inherit Nethercraig or because she had been forced into commitment by the codicil to Hunter's will.

In spite of what had happened between them during the night she still distrusted him because he had managed to avoid discussing the matter with her, and had refused to say what he had in mind to do after they had inherited the property.

Fiona had said he had talked about divorce in two or three years. The coffee percolator filled, Elizabeth plugged it in and then began to search for something to cook for breakfast. She would have to ask Dugald outright about divorce, because if that was what he intended to do in the future she was not going to swear she would stay married to him today. If they were going to split it had to be done soon.

In the hall the telephone bell rang imperatively and automatically she moved towards the door in answer to its summons. It was the second time it had rung within the last fifteen minutes. The first time Dugald had answered it and since he hadn't told her who had rung she had assumed the call had been unimportant.

When she reached the telephone table Dugald was already there, fully dressed, the receiver wedged between his ear and his shoulder as he scribbled something on a notepad. Hearing her approach, he looked at her, his eyes hard and cold.

'Wait a minute,' he said crisply into the mouthpiece. 'She's here now. You'd best speak to her yourself.' He lowered the receiver from his ear and handed it out to her, his mouth curling contemptuously. 'It's your lover-boy,' he drawled, and dropping the receiver into her outstretched hand, he turned and went up the stairs.

'Alan?' Elizabeth exclaimed as she sank down on to the hall chair. 'Where are you?'

'Much closer than you'd guess, darling,' he replied with a chuckle. 'At the Castle Craig Hotel, as a matter of fact.'

'But what are you doing there? I thought you were going right back to Brancaster yesterday.'

'I managed to persuade Dad to stay over another night. Elizabeth, I'd like you and Dad to meet. I was just leaving a message inviting you to come and have lunch with us today here at the hotel.'

'But I have to go to the solicitors today—I told you yesterday.'

'I know you did, but you'd have time for a bar lunch with us before you go.'

'I haven't time, Alan. Thank you very much for the invitation, but please excuse me.'

'Then we'll see you after you've been to the solicitors,' he said, and even over the phone she could sense his urgency. 'I think you said the office is in Duncraig.'

'Yes, I did, in the Town Hall building.'

'We'll wait for you there. I don't suppose you'll be with the solicitor for much more than an hour. And then if you're ready to leave we'll drive you back to Brancaster. You're expected back at the library tomorrow, you know.'

'Yes, I know, but I'm not sure whether all the business to do with Hunter's affairs will be settled this afternoon.'

'You're not the executor, are you?'

'No, Dugald is.'

'Then let him do it all. It's his job. We'll be waiting for you.'

He rang off and Elizabeth put down the receiver, looking down at what Dugald had written on the notepad. She read:

'Message for Liz. Lunch at Castle Craig, twelve-thirty, Fawley.'

Above that he had made some note, presumably after the first phone call. He had written;

'Meet F. at Glasgow Airport five-thirty today. Catch shuttle flight to London. Stay overnight at Hilton. Meeting with K. 9 a.m. sharp tomorrow morning. Make reservation for return flight to Montreal next day with F.'

The aroma of coffee reminded her that it would be perking and she hurried through to the kitchen. 'Meet F. at Glasgow Airport.' Who was F.? F for Fiona? Possibly. He was going away today. Would he tell her when he came downstairs or would he leave it until the last minute, when the meeting with Mr Bothwell was over? Would he invite her to go with him? She was scrambling eggs, which was all there seemed to be in the house to eat, when Dugald came into the room.

'Are you going?' he asked laconically, going over to a cupboard where the dishes were kept and taking out two mugs.

'Going where?' she asked.

'To lunch with lover-boy and your prospective father-in-law.'

'Alan is not my lover!' she snapped furiously, swinging round to face him. He was wearing a well-cut suit of light grey with a crisp white shirt and a dark red tie. He looked unusually elegant and quite suavely businesslike. He seemed like someone she didn't know and had never met before. 'And wherever did you get the idea that Alan's father is going to be my father-in-law?' she demanded.

'From Fawley himself, when I went to see him in hospital,' he replied coldly, pouring coffee hot and black into a mug. 'He told me that once you've divorced me you and he are going to be married.'

'And you believed him?' she gasped.

'I saw no reason not to,' he replied with a shrug of his broad shoulders, and picking up the mug of coffee he went and sat down at the table. He drank some of the liquid, then looked across at her. The wintry bleakness of his eyes as their glance swept over her chilled her to the marrow. What had happened to the passionate yet gentle lover she had known during the night and the first few hours of the morning?

'But . . . but . . . surely last night . . .' she began, her hands twisting round the back of the chair. Then she broke off, biting her lip, recalling her own words about not expecting commitment from him just because they had made love together.

'Last night was an aberration on your part, I suspect,' Dugald said dryly. 'The result of drinking too much sherry, I would guess,' he added, his mouth twitching briefly with amusement. 'A one-night stand, that committed neither of us to anything. I have to go to London tonight to meet a business colleague and I'll be flying back to Montreal as soon as I can get a reservation. There's a chance I'll get a seat on tonight's Air Canada flight. If not I'll fly back via Boston the day after tomorrow.' He paused and looked down at the coffee mug. 'You were babbling something about divorce on Friday when we were driving back from Duncraig, if you remember.'

'Yes, I remember,' she whispered, gripping the back of the chair hard.

'I warned Fawley that it might be some time before one could be arranged because of the matter of fulfilling the terms of Hunter's will.' He slanted her a sidelong glance. 'Did he tell you that?'

'Yes, he did.'

'But once a decent period of time has elapsed and as long as you and I don't cohabit I don't see why we shouldn't get a divorce quite easily in eighteen months or a couple of years' time.' He looked past her at the cooker. 'Looks like we're going up in flames any minute now,' he said dryly. 'Something is burning.'

Elizabeth turned quickly back to the stove. The scrambled eggs were a charred mess at the bottom of the saucepan. She turned off the burner and carrying the pan to the sink ran water into it. It sizzled noisily, steam rising up with the smell of burning. Putting the pan down, she took the two pieces of toast which had popped from the toaster, placed more bread in the toaster, put the toast in the toast rack and carried it to the table.

'We'll just have to have toast and marmalade,' she muttered. 'There are no more eggs.'

Elizabeth poured coffee for herself and returned to the table. She felt strangely numb inside. All the lovely glowing feeling she had experienced earlier had evaporated.

'I'm sure Fiona will be a much more efficient housewife than I am,' she said coolly as she took one of the pieces of toast and scraped butter on to it.

'That wouldn't be hard to achieve,' Dugald retorted tauntingly. 'But why are you forever bringing Fiona into our discussion?'

'Is it a discussion?' she countered. 'I've been getting the impression that you've made up your mind what it is you're going to do and as usual you're expecting me to go along with you. Well, I'm not going to!'

In the process of spreading marmalade on his toast he looked up sharply to frown at her.

'Aren't you? Why not?'

'Because I can't help you carry out the terms of Hunter's will. I can't lie and cheat, like you can. And I can't wait that long for a divorce. I want one as soon as possible. If . . . if you hadn't come here, if . . . if you'd stayed away from me another six months we . . . we could have been divorced in September quite easily. Now . . . now I suppose I'll have to sue you for one on the ground of incompatibility or something.' She sprang to her feet, aware that she might burst into tears and not wanting to break down in front of him. 'I'm not going with you to Mr Bothwell's office this afternoon to swear that I'm going to stay married to you. I'm ... I'm going back to Brancaster with Alan and his father!'

She rushed out into the hall, knuckling away the tears which began to drip from her eyes. Picking up the telephone receiver, she dialled the Castle Craig number quickly, noticing that Dugald's suitcases were by the front door. He was packed and ready to leave. He'd had his one-night stand with her and was going on his way. Oh, God, why did he have the power to hurt her so much? Why had she let him get beneath her skin again?

A voice spoke in her ear and she asked to speak to Mr Fawley senior, thinking it would be easier for Alan's father to get the phone than Alan on his crutches. In a few moments a smooth voice with a north-country accent spoke to her.

'Mr Fawley, this is Elizabeth Morin. I find that I'm able to get away from here sooner than I had expected and I was wondering if the invitation to lunch with you and Alan is still open.'

'Of course it is. We'll be delighted to see you. Now can I come and pick you up? Alan says your house isn't very far from here.'

'Could you? Oh, that would be very helpful.' She gave him instructions on how to get to Nethercraig, and he promised to be there in fifteen minutes and rang off.

Elizabeth replaced the receiver and looked up. Dugald had come into the hall. Hands in his trouser pockets, he was leaning a shoulder against the wall near the telephone table and was watching her. His face was rather pale and his eyes lacked their usual brightness.

'I hope you know what you're doing,' he said quietly.

'Yes, I do,' she replied, her head going up, the pride of the red-haired Finleys showing in every line of her body and in the sparkle of her green eyes. 'I'm doing what I know to be right.'

'This place, Hunter's last will and testament, mean nothing to you, then?' he accused sharply.

'They do mean something to me, but not as much . . . not as much as being married for love means to me,' she replied shakily. 'And I know Hunter wouldn't have approved if . . . if I'd lied just so that we could carry out the terms of his will.'

Her voice choked on the last words and whirling round she ran quickly up the stairs.

CHAPTER SEVEN

IN the bedroom Elizabeth flung off her dressing gown and searched for clothes, deciding to wear the black suit she had worn for the funeral and to team it this time with a lavender-coloured blouse. When she was dressed she wound her thick hair into a knot on top of her head and applied a little make-up to her face. Then snatching her clothing from the wardrobe and from the drawers where she had stored it she began to ram it into her suit-case, not caring if anything was creased in the process. She intended to be ready by the time Alan's father arrived and to go with him immediately, no matter what Dugald said or did to stop her . . . that was if he said or did anything to stop her, she added rather forlornly, because she had a feeling he wouldn't.

Once everything was packed she slung her black woollen coat about her shoulders and went downstairs. As soon as she reached the hallway she noticed that Dugald's cases had gone. Going straight to the front door, she swung it open and went out on to the top step. The little orange car had gone too. He had left without saying goodbye, walking out of her life casually and without regrets, it seemed.

Her ears picked up the sound of a car's engine and in a few seconds the bonnet of a blue car appeared cautiously round the bend in the drive. The car stopped at the bottom of the steps and a man got out of it. He was slim and slight and had greying fair hair and he was dressed smartly in a fawn suit. There was no doubt he was Alan's father. He had the same colouring and as he came up the steps towards her the same hazel eyes looked at her.

'Elizabeth?' he queried, smiling at her, showing well-kept even teeth and holding out his right hand.

'That's right,' she said, shaking his hand. She didn't like the lax, light grip of it and withdrew her own hand quickly.

'I'm Ted Fawley.' His smile grew more obviously charming and the hazel eyes looked right into hers, suggestively. 'And I must say I'm very pleased to meet you, very pleased indeed.'

'Thank you,' she said coolly. 'Can I put my case in the boot, please? Alan said I could go with you when you return to Brancaster.'

'Certainly you can,' he said heartily, and taking the case from her went down the steps with it. He opened the boot, put the case in and closed the boot with a clang. 'It's a lovely place you have here,' he said, turning to her as she went down the steps. 'Alan tells me your father's cousin died recently and left it to you in his will.'

'Only if I obey certain conditions,' she replied stiffly, wishing now that she hadn't told Alan anything about Hunter's will.

'Well, you'd be foolish not to obey them,' said Ted Fawley with that toothy smile of his, a smile which she noticed didn't touch his eyes at all.

They remained still and watchful, reminding her for some reason of a snake's. 'It's one of those places you dream about, that you think of buying if you should be so lucky as to win the football pools or back an outsider to win the Derby or the Grand National,' he added. He turned to the car and opened the door on the passenger side. 'Are you ready to go, now?' he asked.

'I ... I'd better lock the front door first,' she said, going back up the steps and searching in her handbag for the big front door key. What was she going to do with the key? Where should she leave it? Did Dugald have a key? Was the back door locked? Oh, heavens, there were suddenly so many responsibilities! Always when she had left Nethercraig before Hunter had been here, or Jane Brodie. Now there was no one, not even Jim Crosbie the gardener or Bob Morton the chauffeur. Where were they? She realised suddenly she hadn't seen either the gardener or the chauffeur since Dugald had come. Had he told them both to take a holiday as he had told Jane?

'I'll have to make sure the back door is locked too,' she explained, looking back at Ted Fawley.

'Take your time, take your time,' he said good-naturedly. 'With a view like that to look at I could stay here for ever.' He waved a hand in the direction of the silvery shining waters of the Firth.

Elizabeth hurried through the house to the kitchen and out into the back porch. The door was unfastened, so she bolted it from inside, then closed the back door of the kitchen and locked it with its key which she hung on a hook at the back of the door. Going back into the kitchen, she realised she hadn't cleared away the mugs and plates she and Dugald had used at breakfast time. Her mug was still half full of cold coffee and her piece of toast was untouched. Dugald had eaten only half his toast. Hastily she collected everything up, scraped the toast and crumbs from the plates into the garbage bin under the sink, rinsed the mugs and the plates and left them to drain.

It was when she was turning the big key in the lock of the front door that it occurred to her that this might be the last time she saw Nethercraig. If she didn't agree to stay married to Dugald the codicil would come into effect and the house would be sold. Tears brimmed in her eyes and she was forced to sniff and swallow hard to prevent them from falling. She turned the key with a click, withdrew it and put it under the sisal outdoor mat on the top step. She would write to Mr Bothwell and inform him of its whereabouts later.

Ted Fawley had walked over to the edge of the lawn and was staring at the view. She crossed the driveway to join him.

'I see you can get to that island on foot or by car when the tide is out,' he said when he heard her approaching. 'There's someone going out there now.'

Elizabeth looked down over the green flatness of the lawn to the curving shape of the causeway, which looked like the pale stem supporting the green, pink and yellow blossom which was the island. Along that stem an orange-coloured bug, something like a ladybird, was crawling. It was the car Dugald had rented.

'Shall we give chase?' asked Ted Fawley, in a

rallying tone. 'Or do you recognise the car?'

'I recognise it,' she said. 'It's all right, he's not a trespasser.'

Why on earth was Dugald going to the island again? she wondered as she took the seat next to Ted Fawley in the car. Had he, like her, realised this might be the last time he would be at Nethercraig? Had he gone to say goodbye to a place he liked very much, perhaps to say goodbye to a dream he had once experienced? The same dream she had known, the dream of loving and living together for ever.

The bushes that edged the driveway blurred before Elizabeth's eyes as she stared out of the car window. Dugald had accused her of killing one of his dreams when she had refused to go with him to Canada, two and a half years ago. Her lips trembled and she pulled them into a fierce tight line. He had done some shattering of her illusions about him, too. She wasn't entirely to blame for what had gone wrong between them. She had loved him with all her heart and had been prepared to go on loving him for the rest of her life, only she had found out from Fiona that he had deceived her.

'Alan has talked a lot about you,' Ted Fawley's voice interrupted her thoughts. 'And I must say you live up to his description, in looks at any rate,' he added gallantly, giving her one of his over-charming smiles.

He probably smiled like that at all his customers, she thought, when he was trying to make a sale. She knew that he was a sales manager for a well-known cosmetics manufacturer and was responsible for the whole of the north of England. He had always been 'on the road', Alan had told her, and had spent a lot of time away from home, especially during Alan's childhood.

'He tells me he'd like to marry you, but that's out of the question until your divorce is through. Any idea when that will be?'

'I'm going to start proceedings as soon as I get back to Brancaster,' she replied woodenly.

'In that case it shouldn't take too long, provided the other party doesn't take it into his head to counter-sue. You and Alan will have to keep out of each other's way for a while, at least until the decree is granted.'

'Why?' she asked.

'Well, we wouldn't like your present husband to file a counter-suit on the grounds of adultery, would we now?' he said in his smooth oily way. 'Alan's mother wouldn't like that,' he added. 'In fact she doesn't like him having anything to do with you at all. It's not what she'd planned for her beloved only son.'

'What isn't?'

'His marriage to a divorcee,' he said as he turned the car off the road and into the driveway of Castle Craig. 'No, Doreen doesn't like the idea of Alan marrying you one little bit,' he continued. 'That's why I'm glad to have this private chat with you, to warn you what's in store for you when you meet Doreen. She's got it in for you and no mistake.' He slanted her a sly glance. 'You know what some women are like about their sons?'

'No, as a matter of fact I don't,' she replied.

The only mother of a son she had been able to observe at close quarters had been Kirsty, Dugald's mother, that calm, clear-sighted, grey-eyed woman who had loved her only son so much she had been able to release him from her apron strings at an early age.

'They can be damned possessive and live their lives for them. Sometimes their sons mean more to them than their husbands.' Ted Fawley's voice was bitter, and Elizabeth gave him a quick glance. Did Alan mean more to Mrs Fawley than her husband? 'Doreen would like to choose Alan's wife for him,' he continued. 'She'd like him to marry a nice pretty young virgin who hasn't known any men before meeting Alan. Secondhand goods aren't good enough for him, in her opinion. Do you get my meaning?'

'Yes, I get your meaning,' Elizabeth said coldly.

He had stopped the car in the hotel courtyard and had turned off the ignition. Turning to her, he patted her hand where it lay on her knee. Slowly his fingers squeezed hers and then they slid as if by accident slyly over her knee and down her leg before moving away.

'I can see you're intelligent,' he said. 'I couldn't have told you about Doreen if I hadn't noticed that. But forewarned is forearmed, as they say. Think you'll be able to cope with her now?'

'I'll do my best,' she retorted. 'But what about you, Mr Fawley? Haven't you any objection to your only son wanting to marry a woman who's already been married?'

'Not on your life! Not when she's a good-looker

like you are.' It seemed to her that his smile became a leer as once again he squeezed her hand. 'I think you and I are going to get along extremely well, my dear—extremely well indeed,' he murmured, leaning closer so that she felt his breath on her cheek. 'The fact that you're married means you know about the facts of life, and to me that makes you all the more interesting. I'm looking forward to the time when you and Alan move into that house down there and you invite me to come and stay with you. We could have a lot of fun together, you and I, Elizabeth.'

'I think we'd better go in,' she said, opening the door and sliding away from him. 'Alan will be wondering where we are.'

She didn't wait for him. Slamming the car door shut, she walked quickly to the front door of the hotel and was quite relieved to find Alan waiting there, swinging about impatiently on his crutches. His endearing smile which she was glad to see did not resemble his father's lit up his face when he saw her and hobbled over to kiss her cheek before she could prevent him.

'I'm glad you changed your mind,' he said. 'I've ordered our lunch, so it should be ready. I thought you might like the chicken and vegetable soup and some potted shrimp sandwiches. You see how well I know your tastes in food?'

'Thank you,' she said, moving in the direction of the bar as she heard the door behind her open and Ted Fawley come in.

'Elizabeth is coming to Brancaster with us, lad,' he announced as he caught up with them.

'After you've seen the solicitor, you mean?'

asked Alan as they moved across to a table.

'I'm not going to Mr Bothwell's office after all,' she said, taking a chair. Alan manoeuvred himself into the chair beside her and his father took the crutches from him to lean them against the wall.

'Not going? Why not?' Alan queried.

'I decided to leave Dugald to handle everything,' she replied.

'Great! You know, I had a feeling everything was going to turn out right when I woke up this morning.' He turned to Ted enthusiastically. 'Well, what do you think of her, Dad?' he asked.

'She'll do,' said Ted, sitting down and winking at Elizabeth across the table. 'Now all you have to do is convince your mother.'

'Oh, Mum will come round to my way of thinking. She always does,' said Alan with all the confidence of a son who knows he can do no real wrong in his mother's eyes.

'It's a pity Doreen didn't come up here with me,' said Ted. 'If she could see Elizabeth's house she'd soon change her tune. I hope you have a photo of it to show her when we get to Brancaster tonight, Elizabeth. Knowing you're going to inherit a place like that will make her realise, as it's made me realise, that you have independent means and you're not making up to Alan just because he has a good job and a good salary.'

'Liza hasn't made up to me. I've done all the chasing, Dad,' said Alan. 'Haven't I, love?' he added, turning to her, his golden eyes worshipping her and embarrassing her with their drank reverence.

The conversation was making her feel sick, but

she couldn't think how to get out of going to Brancaster with them now that her suitcase was in the boot of Ted's car. And anyway, she wanted to go to Brancaster to prove to Dugald that she wasn't going to stay married to him just to benefit from Hunter's will. Once she was on her own ground, in her own flat, she could close the door on the Fawleys, son as well as father. She could close the door on Dugald too. She could be her own person, free as a bird, beholden to no one.

'When do you think you'll be able to return to work, Alan?' she asked, changing the subject. 'Did they tell you at the hospital when you can go back?'

'I'm supposed to wait until the leg is almost healed,' he replied. 'As soon as I can I'll go to Brancaster General and get the orthopaedic man there to look at it and X-ray it, and he'll tell me when I can return to the library.'

'I wouldn't rush back if I were you,' she cautioned. 'Take all the time off you can.'

'That's what I've been telling him,' said Ted. 'And you can be sure Doreen will say the same. She'll want to fuss over him.'

Their soup arrived. Elizabeth ate hungrily, wondering if Dugald was on his way back across the causeway. Regret gnawed at her. She wished she was with him just as she had wished yesterday. She could have gone with him if she hadn't decided to come here for lunch and together they could have been cut off by the tide; together they could have resurrected the dream they had shared once, of loving and living together, of sharing. . . . Oh, what was the use of thinking about it? If

Dugald had wanted her to go with him to the island he would have asked her. But he didn't want her with him all the time. He liked to go about on his own. All he wanted from a woman was that she should be there when he returned to his home, to share his bed, but not to share his thoughts, or his work, to keep house for him and raise his children.

Supposing she had his child as a result of what had happened the previous night? It was possible. Children were often born of such intensely passionate and satisfying unions, and neither of them had taken precautions. She glanced at Alan, who was talking to his father. Would he want to marry her if she were carrying another man's child? Her glance strayed on to Ted Fawley's weak yet sensual face. Would he like the idea of his son having to support another man's child? And what about the formidable Doreen Fawley? Elizabeth bent her head to hide a smile. In a way she was looking forward to meeting Doreen. The woman sounded as if she had a mind of her own, even if she was possessive about Alan. And why shouldn't she worry about his choice of a wife? He was her child and as a good mother she would want him to be happy. She wouldn't want him destroyed by a woman who didn't really care for him. She wouldn't want his dream shattered. Elizabeth bit her lip, thinking again of Dugald whose dream she had shattered.

'If it's all right with you two I'd like to get on the road as soon as possible,' said Ted, rising to his feet. 'So I'll just pay up here and fetch our cases down. I'll see you both at the car in about ten minutes.'

He left the bar room, and Alan turned to Elizabeth with a sigh of relief.

'Now I can ask you. Have you talked about a divorce with Morin?'

'Yes, I have mentioned it.'

'And?'

'I'm going to file for a divorce as soon as I get back to Brancaster.'

'As soon as that?' His eyebrows shot up in surprise. 'But I thought . . . he said you'd have to wait until the terms of Mr Finley's will were fulfilled.'

'I'm not going to wait. I've decided not to abide by the conditions Hunter set down in his will,' said Elizabeth.

'But doesn't that mean you won't inherit the house?' Alan's voice rose a little and several people looked round at him.

'Shhh!' Elizabeth warned him. 'Let's not talk about it here. Mr Arnott, the manager, knows me and I don't want the news spreading around the neighbourhood yet. Let's go out now. Your father will be ready and waiting for us.'

Alan sat in the back seat of the car so that he could put his injured leg up and Elizabeth had to sit next to Ted. Determined not to be drawn into any conversation with either father or son, she pretended to be sleepy. Folding her coat up, she wedged it between the back of the seat and the window and, resting her head against it, closed her eyes. Once on the road, however, Ted Fawley wasted no time. He was a good fast driver and it wasn't long before they were passing through

Dumfries and making for the road to Carlisle. Once they had reached the Border city Elizabeth knew they would take the motorway to Brancaster and would reach the university town by five o'clock at the latest.

As it was, the fingers on the clock of one of Brancaster's more important churches were pointing to quarter past five when Ted turned the car down a street of pleasant semi-detached brick houses and stopped before number eighty-one.

'You'll come and meet Mother, please?' Alan whispered to her from the back seat.

'All right,' she agreed reluctantly, and was at his side when the black front door opened and Mrs Fawley appeared.

Much to Elizabeth's surprise Doreen Fawley was not tall and stately as she had imagined her to be but was a small neat woman with fine features and mousy brown hair which had been carefully set by a hairdresser. There was a discontented droop to her mouth and her brown eyes looked strained and anxious. But her whole face lit up when she saw Alan and she stepped straight up to him and put her arms about him.

'Ah, poor lamb!' she crooned. 'Have you been in much pain? Here, let me help you.'

'I'm all right, Mother. I can manage fine on the crutches. I'd like you to meet Elizabeth Morin who works with me in the library and whom I'm going to marry one day. Liza, this is my mother.'

Elizabeth had to give Doreen Fawley credit for having some pride and good manners. After hugging Alan and kissing his cheek, his mother turned to Elizabeth and held out her hand.

'How do you do, Mrs Morin,' she said politely, and perhaps there was just the suspicion of emphasis on the word *Mrs*. 'Alan had told me a lot about you. Won't you come in and have some tea? I've put the kettle on. It won't take long to boil.'

'Er—thank you. I don't want to put you to any trouble,' Elizabeth began.

'Of course she's going to have tea with us,' said Ted Fawley heartily. 'Come on, Elizabeth, let me take your coat.' His hands rested heavily and meaningfully on her shoulders and she saw Doreen's brown eyes narrow suspiciously, so she slipped from under the coat as quickly as she could. Of the Fawley parents she was fast coming to the conclusion that she preferred the mother to the father.

'I'll take your coat upstairs to the bedroom,' said Doreen, taking the coat from Ted. 'I expect you'd like to wash your hands, Mrs Morin?'

'Elizabeth, please,' said Elizabeth. 'Yes, I would like to visit the bathroom.'

'Then come with me.'

Elizabeth followed her up the stairs and into a small single bedroom at the front of the house. As soon as they were in the room Doreen tossed the coat down on the bed and going over to the door closed it. Turning, she faced a surprised Elizabeth, who was feeling as if she had been very neatly caught and imprisoned and was now facing a formidable gaoler.

'I'm not pleased, you know, not a bit pleased by what our Alan said down there,' said Doreen, drawing herself up to her full height and looking Elizabeth in the eyes. 'And if I have my way he's not going to marry a divorcee. He had a nice girlfriend, Susan Brand, before he took a fancy to you. She'd make him a good wife. She'd look after him and. . . .'

'Take over where you leave off, I'm sure,' put in Elizabeth irrepressibly.

'What did you say?' Doreen seemed to bristle.

'Not very much. I was only agreeing with you that Alan needs someone to look after him, to show him the way. To see that he changes his socks regularly, has clean clothes to wear and eats the right food,' said Elizabeth softly.

'You're right there,' agreed Doreen, the wind taken out of her sails, the anxious look returning to her face. 'You've no idea how absentminded he is! I think he'd starve to death if I didn't make sure the food was on the table for him. His head is in the clouds all the time. He's always thinking about books and about comparing editions of ancient publications; or about digging up the past.'

'I know. He's a very good librarian and is extremely knowledgeable about books. He's doing really well at his job,' said Elizabeth.

'Well, it's kind of you to say so.' Doreen was almost smiling.

'And I can understand why you think he shouldn't marry yet, and I'd like you to know that whole idea is his, not mine. He's so impetuous.'

'Don't you want to marry him, then?' demanded Doreen, sharply.

'I'm still married and I'm not sure when I'll get a divorce. And even if I am divorced I'm not sure I'll want to marry again in a hurry,' murmured Elizabeth. 'Divorce is . . . a very traumatic experience and I expect it will be some time before I'll be able to think of marrying anyone else and adjusting to another man in my life. I expect I'll have to go away for a while, perhaps change my job.' Elizabeth glanced at Doreen warily. 'I haven't told Alan this yet. You see, I don't want to hurt his feelings.'

'He's not good enough for you. Is that it?' said Doreen with a touch of belligerence.

'No, no, it isn't that.'

'Oh, you needn't deny it. I wasn't born yesterday. I can guess Alan doesn't measure up in your eyes to the man you've got already. So why are you getting a divorce?' demanded Doreen, still aggressive.

'That isn't any of your business,' retorted Elizabeth.

'Perhaps you're right, it isn't,' agreed Doreen with surprising equanimity. 'I'd best go and see to the bacon and egg pie I've made for tea. It should be cooked by now. The bathroom is the first door on your left. We'll be in the dining room when you come down.' She paused in the doorway and gave Elizabeth what could only be described as a motherly glance. 'You're a good-looking lass,' she added. 'And I think it's a pity you can't hang on to the man you've got. But then, on the other hand, perhaps you'll be better off without him. I know that if things had been different in my day . . . I mean if divorce had been easier, I wouldn't be here now, tied to that . . . that lecher downstairs!'

She went out of the room and Elizabeth stood listening to her retreating footsteps, astonished by what Doreen had said about her husband. She had a feeling that if they had met under different circumstances she and Doreen could have been friends, in the same way she and Alan were friends. Going into the bathroom, she rinsed her hands quickly and dried them, then went down to the small overcrowded dining room to take her place at the table.

The high tea which Doreen provided was excellent in its north-country way. The pastry of the bacon and egg pie was crisp and crunchy and the filling the right consistency and properly seasoned. A lettuce and tomato salad was served with it. Afterwards there was home-made fruit cake, heavy with raisins, currants and cherries, and soft creamy scones to eat with home-made blackcurrant jam. The conversation was fairly light and general until Ted Fawley mentioned Nethercraig.

'You should see the place, Doreen. It's the sort of house you often read about in books or see on the telly, one of those Scottish stately homes, standing by itself in acres of gardens with a view across the water . . .'

'When you can see it, that is,' put in Elizabeth with dry humour, looking at Doreen. 'When it isn't raining.'

'And Elizabeth is going to inherit it,' added Ted.

'No, she isn't,' said Alan.

'What did you say?' exclaimed Ted.

'I said Liza isn't going to inherit that house because she isn't going to fulfil the conditions laid down by her cousin in his will. She can only inherit it if she stays married to Dugald Morin,' explained Alan.

'Is that true?' Ted demanded.

'Yes, it is,' she replied, returning his cold, suspicious glare serenely.

'And you led me on this morning to believe Alan would be sharing that house with you and Doreen and I would be visiting you there!' he accused.

'I didn't lead you on. You led yourself on,' she replied quietly, and rose to her feet. 'It was a lovely tea, Mrs Fawley, but I think it's time I went to my flat. I have a lot to do to get ready for work in the morning, so if you'll excuse me. . . .'

'Ted will drive you home,' said Doreen, standing up. 'I'll go upstairs and get your coat.'

She left the room and Elizabeth turned towards Ted.

'You don't have to drive me home,' she said. 'I can go by bus if you'll let me have my suitcase.'

'It'll be no trouble,' he said, showing his teeth in a smile she didn't like. 'No trouble at all. I'll go and get the car started.'

He went out, and Alan hobbled across the room on his crutches to accompany her into the hall.

'When will I see you again?' he asked.

'I'm not sure.'

'You'll come and visit me here, while I'm stuck in the house?' he said urgently. 'You must! Mother is likely to drive me round the bend with her fussing.'

She turned to face him, determined to put an end to any further relationship with him. The time had come to make it clear to him that she had no interest in marrying him.

'Your mother isn't at all keen on your friendship with me,' she told him.

'I know. But she'll come round when she gets to know you better,' he wheedled. 'And she will get to know you better over the next few weeks if you'll come every day to see me while I can't go to work.'

'Alan, I think you should take notice of what she says,' she urged. 'You should marry someone who's able to look after you properly, someone who would be more supportive than I would be. She says you had a girl-friend before you met me and. . . .'

'Sue, you mean?' he interrupted her. 'But she's not much more than a child, only just out of her teens.' He stared at her, bewilderment flickering in his eyes. 'Are you trying to tell me you don't want to marry me after all?' he asked in a hoarse whisper.

'I've never said I would marry you,' she replied, also in a whisper, as she heard Doreen coming down the stairs.

'Here's your coat, Elizabeth,' said Doreen, and held the coat out to her. She slipped her arms into the sleeves and turning to Doreen smiled at her.

'Thank you for a lovely tea,' she said. 'And don't worry any more about Alan and me. Goodbye, Mrs Fawley. Goodbye, Alan.'

'But, Elizabeth, you'll call in tomorrow on your way home from work?' Alan called after her as she went out through the front door. 'Please! I'll be expecting you. . . .'

The rest of his words were cut off as Mrs Fawley closed the door after her.

With the approach of evening the fine weather had given way to a thin drizzle of rain falling from a fast darkening sky. Elizabeth's small apartment was in one of the blocks of flats which were situated on the edge of the park not far from the university, and to reach it Ted Fawley had to drive through the middle of the town.

'Well, that was a fine trick you played on me, milady,' he said after they had sat in silence for a while.

'I didn't play any trick on you,' she replied coldly.

'You let me think our Alan had caught an heiress to a fortune!'

'Your Alan hasn't caught anyone. I haven't promised to marry him.'

'I can see why he's attracted to you,' he went on as he turned his car into the cul-de-sac where the block of flats in which she lived was situated. 'You've got style and a lot of spirit.' He stopped the car outside the block and turned off the ignition. Taking a hand off the steering wheel, he slid it up over her thigh. 'I bet you're good in bed, too. How about you inviting me into your flat for a nightcap?'

'Leave me alone!' she retorted furiously, hitting at his hand with her fist. 'You ... you ... dirty old man!'

'Dirty, am I? Old, am I?' he snarled. 'It seems to me you're in need of a lesson!'

Elizabeth groped frantically for the lever to

open the door, but was too late to avoid him. He grabbed her arm and jerked her against him. Cold and flaccid, his lips covered hers. Using all her strength, she pushed against him, trying to break free. Suddenly the door behind her opened. Ted Fawley raised his head, but his hold on her didn't slacken.

'Who are you? What do you want?' he demanded of whoever had opened the door.

'I'd like to speak to my wife,' replied a deep voice—Dugald's voice. 'Perhaps you wouldn't mind letting go of her so she can get out.'

Ted was so surprised he let go of her quickly and she almost fell backwards.

'Get out, Liza,' Dugald ordered in a cold crisp voice. 'Go and open up your flat. I'll be with you in a few minutes when I've had another word with this guy.'

Elizabeth didn't need to be told twice and she scrambled out to stand beside him on the wet pavement.

'My suitcase is in the boot,' she whispered.

'I'll bring it up.'

'What are you doing here?'

'I'll explain later. Go on, go up to your flat.'

In the light shed from the street lamps she could see his face was set in hard unpleasant lines and that his eyes were glittering frostily.

'You won't . . . you won't hurt him, will you?' she whispered, afraid of the savagery expressed in his face.

'That will depend entirely on him,' he replied softly. 'Go on, get inside out of the rain.'

She hurried into the entrance hall, found her

key and opened the main door. Up the stairway she ran to the first floor and along the corridor to her flat. Her hand shaking, she inserted her key into the lock and opened the door.

CHAPTER EIGHT

NEVER had the small living room of her one bedroom flat seemed such a haven to Elizabeth as she stepped into it and closed the door and switched on the light. Favourite pictures, ornaments and pieces of furniture glinted a welcome to her. For a few moments she leaned against the closed door, trying to control the feeling of revulsion which was flooding through her. Would she ever be able to forget the unpleasant touch of Ted Fawley's lips against hers or of his hand on her thigh? God, the memory of what had been happening in the car made her want to throw up! Gagging on the nausea that rose in her throat, she was moving towards the bathroom when the buzzer sounded, indicating that someone wanted to enter the main door of the flats and come up to see her. Cautiously she lifted the receiver off the wall.

'Who is it?' she asked.

'Dugald. I have your suitcase.'

She pressed the button which would release the lock on the door downstairs and hung up the receiver. In a few minutes Dugald would be in the room. Her hands went to her hot cheeks. She could hardly believe he was here in Brancaster. Why was he here? Why hadn't he gone to Glasgow Airport to meet Fiona? Had he come to spy on her? To watch her behaviour with Alan so he could sue her for divorce? Would Dugald do something like that? Was he so cruel?

She recalled the expression on his face under the street lamp and shivered. He had looked as if he could have strangled her there and then. The doorbell rang suddenly and she jumped, turning to the door, hesitating about opening it. It rang again and the ring was followed by several loud knocks on the door.

'Liza!' Dugald shouted. 'Open up! Liza, are you all right?'

If she didn't answer the door he would disturb everyone in the flats with his shouting and knocking. Quickly she went to the door and opened it. Eyes as clear as iced water glinted down at her from between thick black lashes. His face was taut still, the skin drawn tightly across high cheekbones, his broad-lipped generous mouth set in a narrow line. Raindrops glittered on his black hair. He looked furious in a severely controlled way which somehow made him seem more dangerous, and as he moved forward to enter the room Elizabeth backed away from him nervously.

He slammed the door shut and dropped her case to the floor, and they stood staring at each other in a tense silence.

'How . . . how did you get here?' she asked at last, her voice not much more than a croak. It was rather a foolish question, but she was still amazed that he was there with her and not in London with Fiona.

'By car,' he replied tersely.

'But . . . but . . . I thought you were going to London?' she whispered.

'I changed my mind.' He was still curt and still looking at her as if he would like to hurt her in some way.

'How ... how long have you been here?' she asked nervously, turning away from him.

'About an hour. I've been waiting for you to turn up. Where have you been?'

'We ... I was invited to tea by Alan's mother,' she replied. 'Then ... then Mr Fawley offered to drive me home.'

'Mr Fawley?' he exclaimed. 'You mean that guy out there was Alan's father?'

'Yes,' she muttered.

'My God!' His voice thickened with disgust. 'Why couldn't you have waited until you were both inside the flat before you gave him a come-on signal?'

'I didn't give him any come-on signal!' she hissed at him angrily. 'Oh, how could you say that? How dare you say it? How dare you even think it about me!' Suddenly for some reason she was crying. Tears were pouring down her cheeks and noisy sobs were shaking her. Her hands over her face, she struggled to control herself, but couldn't. Dugald's suggestion that she had deliberately invited Ted Fawley to kiss and fondle her was the last straw. She felt beaten and battered, tired of coping, tired of dealing with men and their irrational, often infuriating behaviour.

'I'm sorry, Liza.' He sounded quite humble for once and spoke just behind her. 'I guess I was out of line in saying that about you.' She heard his breath hiss as he drew it in sharply. 'The truth is, something happened to me when I saw what was going on in that car. I seemed to explode inside. If you'd been with Alan I might not have felt quite so savage, perhaps, knowing how fond you are of him. But to see you with an absolute stranger, old enough to be your father. . . .' he broke off as his voice choked with disgust again. 'I could have strangled him there and then for touching you,' he said thickly. 'I could have strangled you too, for letting him.'

'I did not let him!' she flared, swinging round to face him. 'And you should know enough about me by now to realise that I would never deliberately invite a strange man to maul me. He . . . he . . . oh, he was horrible!' she gasped, hands at her cheeks again. 'Ever since we met when he came to Castle Craig he's been making up to me suggestively. He seemed to think that because I'd been married and might soon be divorced I . . . I'd be free and easy, and when I refused to invite him into the flat and told him to leave me alone he said I needed teaching a lesson for . . . for leading him on, and so he . . . he attacked me. I tried to break free, but I couldn't.' Her mouth trembled. 'Oh, Dugald,' she whispered, 'I've never been so glad to hear or see anyone as I was to hear and see you. I don't care why you came here this evening. I'm just glad that you did.'

Her hands reached out to him. He took them in his and drew her gently into the shelter of his arms. Closing her eyes, she laid her head against his chest, letting his warmth and strength comfort her. For a while they stood like that, not speaking or moving, content for those few moments to be close to each other.

'Feeling better now?' he asked softly at last, his fingers groping for and finding her chin to tip her face upwards. From between reddened eyelids she saw his face slightly out of focus, its angles and lines blurred. It seemed to her that the expression in his eyes was one of sadness.

'Yes, thank you.' She leaned away from him against the arms which now held her loosely. 'Why did you go to Mindoon again today?'

'You saw me going there?' His eyebrows went up in surprise.

'Yes, just before I left Nethercraig.'

'I went over to close the windows I'd left open to air the place yesterday,' he replied coolly, his arms falling away from her to his sides. Thrusting his hands in his pockets, he turned away and sat down in one of the armchairs and stretched his long legs before him.

'You might have asked me to go with you,' Elizabeth challenged him.

'At the time I didn't think you'd be interested in going with me. You were far more interested in going to lunch with Alan and in returning to Brancaster with him, I remember,' he remarked dryly. He gave her a piercing underbrowed look. 'If I'd asked you would you have gone with me?'

She looked down at her hands which for some reason were twisting together. Not liking that betraying movement of nervousness, she separated them and dug them in the pockets of her coat.

'It would have been nice to have been offered the chance to go,' she evaded. 'You haven't asked me to go anywhere with you for a long time.'

'Not for two and a half years, in fact, here in this flat, and you refused.' His mouth curved wryly. 'You could say that experience made me more than wary of asking you to go anywhere with me again. Rejection has a way of stiffening one's defences against further hurt.'

'I didn't know that I had hurt you,' she exclaimed. 'I didn't think I could hurt you, not after what Fiona had told me about you marrying me to please Hunter and so you could benefit from his will. She said she wondered how you could marry me and be in love with another woman. I wondered how you could, too.'

'And which woman did she suggest I was in love with?' Dugald drawled with a touch of mockery.

'She didn't suggest anyone, but at the time I thought she meant you were in love with the woman in Montreal, with Michèle.' She noticed his eyebrows flicker in sceptical amusement and added hurriedly, 'It wasn't until last Friday evening that I realised Fiona meant you were in love with her when I found out you'd been seeing her while we've been separated.'

'I have seen Fiona once since we separated, last September when I was visiting Hunter,' he replied coldly. 'We met in the village outside the post office, if you want to know the exact details. She was with her grandmother. They'd been for a walk. We talked for about ten minutes, then I got into my car to drive down here to see you.' Irony throbbed in his voice. 'It was hardly a meeting between lovers,' he added. 'But she appears to have made the most of it when talking to you. What else has she been saying to you about me?'

'On Sunday she was very upset because you'd told her it would be a while before you and I could get a divorce. She said you'd told her we would have to wait until all the terms of Hunter's will were fulfilled. You told Alan the same thing when you went to see him on Saturday. And you told me that today, if you remember, at breakfast time.'

'I know I did.' Dugald tipped his head back against the back of the chair and looked at her through the veil of his lashes, his eyes glinting with derision. 'Delaying tactics,' he explained, and then sat up suddenly to glare at her. 'You see, I have no intention of letting you divorce me and I have no intention of divorcing you.'

'But ... but you must,' she insisted rather weakly, and sat down suddenly on the cushion-covered stool which acted as a footrest for the armchair.

'Why must I? Why should I make it easy for you to marry Alan?' he rasped.

'I'm not going to marry Alan,' she retorted. 'That was all his idea, not mine, never mine. He's ... he's ... well, all I can say is he's infatuated with me for some reason.'

'Then if you're not going to marry him why all this talk of divorce?' he demanded.

'Because Fiona says she can't wait much longer to marry you. She was in a terrible state yesterday, pleading with me to persuade you to agree to a divorce as soon as possible. She said you were going to sue for divorce anyway, if our separation had lasted another six months . . . and I thought, or at least I'd assumed that was why you'd tried to see me in Brancaster last September.' Her head bowed so that he couldn't see the pain it was causing her to talk about divorce, she licked her lips and added, 'You can't marry her unless we're divorced, and if you think I'm going to put up with her being your mistress, you're quite mistaken. I will never put up with anything like that. Never!' She raised her head to give him a fierce glance.

'You won't have to,' he retorted. 'I've never wanted Fiona to be either my wife or my mistress.'

Elizabeth gaped at him. He was leaning towards her and seated as they were their faces were on a level, so close that she could see dark smudges of weariness beneath his eyes and a bruised look about his high cheekbones. Strain and unhappiness were written on his face quite clearly for her to see and she wondered she had never noticed them before. Perhaps she had never looked before, not so as to see clearly, that was, not with the eyes of love. She had been too busy coping with her own tormented emotions to see that Dugald had been suffering too.

'Then why were you going to meet her at Glasgow Airport today and why had you planned to travel with her to Montreal?' she asked in bewilderment.

His eyes widened and she could see there was a dark edging to the crystal-clear irises which she hadn't noticed before either.

'Where in hell did you get that idea?' he asked.

'From the notepad beside the phone in the hall at Nethercraig. You'd written on it "Meet F. at Glasgow Airport at five-thirty today." And further on there was a reference to arranging a reservation to Montreal for F.'

For a few seconds Dugald stared at her, various expressions chasing across his face ranging from amazement through exasperation to frank amusement.

'If I didn't find it so funny I'd up-end you, put you across my knee and spank you right now,' he growled at her.

'Oh. Why?' She shifted away from him, misjudged the size of the footstool and tipping it over fell off it backwards, her slim legs waving awkwardly in the air as she landed on her back and elbows. From her suddenly inferior position she glared up at him. 'Why?' she demanded. 'Why do you want to spank me? What have I done?'

'Jumped to conclusions far too often,' he grated, and getting to his feet, he towered over her. 'It's time you stopped reading messages which aren't for you and interpreting them wrongly. It's time, too, you stopped listening to Fiona and believing everything she says. It's time you stopped trusting her. It's high time you listened to and believed me.' He poked at his chest with the tip of his right thumb. 'I'm the one you promised to love and cherish. I'm the one you vowed to trust, not Fiona. You believed her two and a half years ago and thought the worst of me. . . .'

'Well, so did you believe what she told you

about me,' she retorted, scrambling to her feet and facing up to him, and he had the grace to look taken aback.

'What did she tell me about you?' he demanded, scowling at her.

'She told you that I'd married you for the same reason that you married me, to please Hunter and to benefit from his will. And you believed her.'

'And didn't you marry me to please Hunter and benefit from his will?' He glared at her accusingly and it occurred to her that they were shouting at each other and that possibly her neighbours would be able to hear through the thin dividing walls of the flats.

But what did it matter if they were shouting? At last they were communicating verbally, telling each other what had been in the depths of their hearts all this time.

'I've told you that, yes, I did marry you to please Hunter, but it wasn't the only reason. And it wasn't because I wanted the benefit from his will,' she replied, lowering her voice.

'Then why?'

'I married you because I loved you and thought I would like to live with you and share everything with you.' She placed her palms against her cheeks, which were flaming. 'Oh, I was very much in love with you that night we spent on Mindoon,' she whispered.

'Was?' Irony crackled in his voice. 'It didn't last long, did it, that feeling of love? And it wasn't strong enough to stand up to the first blast of jealousy. It wasn't love. You'd have trusted me if you'd loved me.' He drew a deep exasperated breath and swung away from her to go and stare out of the uncurtained window at the rain-blurred lights of the town. 'I guess you were too young,' he went on in a low voice. 'Too young for marriage and all that I expected from such a close relationship with you.' He paused, then added slowly, 'That was why I suggested we separated for a while. I thought separation would give you a chance to grow up and find out if marriage and all that it entails was what you really wanted. I knew that both Hunter and your mother had pressured you into marrying me. He wanted to make his dearest wish come true. She wanted to feather her own nest.—Oh, yes,' he said quickly, when Elizabeth would have objected, 'Sandra really did accept money from Hunter to go away for a while and let true love take its own course.' He shrugged his shoulders, his mouth twisting cynically. 'And if I hadn't been so crazy about you by then . . . infatuated, if you like to put it that way . . . I'd have held back and suggested to Hunter that you and I became engaged to be married instead of rushing headlong into that delicate, dangerous arrangement like I did. But I guess I was out of my mind, driven that way temporarily by the desire to possess your tiger-lily beauty.'

His eyes hooded by their heavy lids, he stared at her as if the urge to take her there and then was sweeping through him, and she felt her pulses leap in response to that look of blatant desire. 'I was also very much in love, that summer, with you, although at first I hated you because you could make me feel so uncouth and inferior to you,' he whispered. 'I'm still in love with you. That's why

I'm here and why I didn't go to Glasgow Airport to meet Fred Clarkson.'

'Fred Clarkson?' she repeated dazedly. Had she heard correctly? Had he really said he was still in love with her?

'F is the initial letter of other names besides Fiona,' he mocked as he came across the room to stand before her.

'Who is he?' she asked.

'Another friend of mine from university days and also a geo-physicist. He was at Ian's yesterday. He's been looking for a way to emigrate to Canada and I told him our company could use his expertise. He said he would talk it over with his wife and phone me this morning. When he phoned I arranged to meet him at Glasgow Airport this evening to fly with him to London to introduce him to our personnel manager who's over here interviewing prospective employees for the company. The reference to making a reservation on a flight to Montreal was not for Fiona but for Fred. You jumped to the wrong conclusion, in the same way you did when you read that letter from Michèle.'

'Maybe I wouldn't have done if you hadn't been so cold and nasty at breakfast and if you hadn't talked about getting a divorce in eighteen months' time. If you hadn't. . . .' Elizabeth's voice shook, but she braced her shoulders and glared up at him again, knowing that it all had to come out, the pain and the bitterness, otherwise it would fester in her mind for ever. 'If you hadn't referred to what had happened between us last night as a . . . as a one-night stand,' she finished miserably.

Dugald's glance didn't waver, but an expression

of pain flickered in his eyes and bone showed white along his jaw as he set his teeth.

'I've regretted many of the things I've said to you in the past three days, but none more than that,' he said quietly. Raking a hand through his hair, he paced away from her, stood for a moment with his shoulders hunched as if thinking deeply, then paced back to face her again to look down at her, a tortured expression in his eyes. 'When you hurt me I tend to lash out, to strike back,' he explained. 'Last night you'd spelled it out pretty clearly that by making love with me you didn't feel committed to me in any way, and I know that a woman is just as capable of using a man to get rid of feelings of frustration as a man is capable of using a woman. Then Alan had to phone this morning to ask you to lunch. I was as jealous as hell, so I hit back.' His mouth curved cynically. 'Anyway, you'd already told me you didn't love me and wanted a divorce.'

He shrugged again and walked away to the window. In the silence Elizabeth could hear the faint patter of rain against the pane and the sound of the television in the next flat.

'All we ever seem to do is hurt each other,' she said forlornly. 'And yet . . . I . . . I don't want to hurt you and I don't want to be hurt by you. I suppose it's because I love you that I'm hurt by what you do and what you say.'

He swung round again to face her, his expression unyielding.

'Do you love me?' he challenged.

'I . . . I believed I didn't,' she muttered. 'But . . . but since we've been together again I've found out you were right when you said my feelings for you had been frozen by our separation and once the thaw set in they began to grow again.' She noticed he still looked cynical and something burst within her. 'Oh, why do you think I refused to go with you to Mr Bothwell's office to swear I wanted to stay married to you?' she exploded.

'I supposed it was because you didn't want to swear you would stay married to me,' he replied, his eyebrows tilting in sardonic amusement.

'It was because I love you and I couldn't think of any other way to convince you that I hadn't married you just so that I would benefit from Hunter's will. I thought that if I did swear that I wanted to stay married to you you would think I was only doing it so I could inherit half of Nethercraig and the money he left, and not because I love you,' she explained earnestly.

'I see.' He looked very perplexed. 'I'm afraid the logic of your argument evades me. And your refusal to go with me to see Bothwell again had quite the opposite effect to what you intended. I assumed you were so in love with Alan you would even give up the property and all that Hunter had wanted to leave to you so you could marry him.' Again he rumpled his hair and shook his head. 'I didn't know what to do, how to deal with the new situation you'd created by your refusal. It wasn't until I was on Mindoon again. . . .' He paused and stepped closer to her. Raising a hand, he stroked a strand of her hair back from her cheek, his fingers lingering caressingly about her throat. 'Remember the night we spent in the cottage?' he murmured.

'I've never forgotten it,' she whispered.

'I thought about it on Sunday when I was on the island. That's why I left the windows open to air the place. I thought that when I'd brought you back from the hospital we would go over there together at the next low tide that night and stay there, get things straightened out between us before going to see Bothwell the next day.' His hand fell to his side and his mouth twisted wryly. 'But that dream was shattered too, because when I arrived at the hospital you'd gone to Brancaster, or so I believed.' He sighed heavily.

'We've always seemed to be at cross-purposes,' Elizabeth whispered.

'And yet we had so much going for us three years ago,' he mused. 'It was when I was closing the windows of the cottage today that I began to wonder where we'd gone wrong and I decided we hadn't had enough time alone together. Even this past weekend there've been interruptions all the time. And there I was letting you go away, back to Brancaster. I left the rest of the windows open and drove straight to the hotel immediately, to stop you from going with the Fawleys. When I got there Jack Arnott told me you'd just left.'

'Oh, I wish you'd come sooner, I wish you'd come sooner,' she groaned.

'I drove to Duncraig, told Bothwell we wanted another few days before signing anything before witnesses, phoned Fred to tell him to go to London by himself and then set off in hot pursuit of you.' He grinned suddenly. 'Jealous husband drives to rescue wife from her knight errant,' he mocked.

'I'm so glad you came to rescue me,' she whispered, and raising her hands she framed his face with them and drew his head down until their lips touched. At once his arms went round her in the bear-like hug which always made her feel so helpless. Hard and hot, his lips seared hers as if he wanted to burn away for ever the cold licentious touch of Ted Fawley's lips.

'Love makes the difference,' she whispered in his ear as they stood for a moment cheek to cheek when the kiss was over.

'To what?'

'To the way I feel when *you* are holding and kissing me and to the way you hold and kiss *me*.'

'And that's something else you've learned since you've been married to me,' Dugald taunted softly. 'I've learned something too, since I've been married to you,' he added, pushing her away from him so he could look into her eyes.

'Oh? What?'

'I've learned that there's much more pleasure in taking if I do some giving first,' he whispered, tilting her lips to his again, and for a while there was silence.

'Do you want to stay here tonight?' he asked a little later.

'I want to stay wherever you want to be,' Elizabeth replied hazily.

'I'd like to go back to Nethercraig. Will you come with me, please, Liza?'

'Now?'

'Now.' He was suddenly autocratic again, organising her life for her. 'We can be there in about three hours, in time to catch low tide. We can cross to the island and spend the night in the cottage as I'd planned. Would you like that?'

'I'd *love* that,' she replied fervently. 'I was beginning to think you'd never ask me to go there again with you. How long will we stay?'

'For as long as we like, for ever if we want,' he replied with a touch of that bold extravagance which was so much a part of his nature.

'But what about your business in Canada? What about the company?'

'That can look after itself until we've mended our dreams and made Hunter's dream come true,' he replied, and once more she was swept into his arms and was kissed mercilessly.

It was almost one o'clock in the morning when the tyres of the orange car crunched cautiously over the shingle and mud causeway to Mindoon. In the moonlight the sea and the mudbanks shimmered with silvery radiance. It was a night to remember, thought Elizabeth dreamily, like last night and like other nights she had shared with Dugald. And as long as they shared nights like this to remember in the future together how could they go wrong?

They reached the end of the causeway and the car climbed up a slope and turned on to the narrow grassy track which twisted round to the other side of the island. In a few minutes they stopped outside a small whitewashed cottage. Hand in hand they walked to the doorway, Dugald put down their cases and felt for the key which was always left on a ledge above the door. He found it, turned it in the lock and pushed the door open. Elizabeth stepped forward, but his hand on her arm held her back. She turned to him enquiringly.

'Let's do it properly. We're beginning our marriage all over again, so let's start it in the right way,' he said, and sliding one arm about her shoulders and the other beneath her knees he lifted her and carried her across the threshold.

ROMANCE

Variety is the spice of romance

Each month, Mills & Boon publish new romances. New stories about people falling in love. A world of variety in romance — from the best writers in the romantic world. Choose from these titles in March.

STORMY VIGIL Elizabeth Graham
LAW OF THE JUNGLE Mary Wibberley
THE GOLDEN SPANIARD Rebecca Stratton
THE TRODDEN PATHS Jacqueline Gilbert
MAN OF TEAK Sue Peters
STAMP OF POSSESSION Sheila Strutt
LOVE'S DUEL Carole Mortimer
JUDITH Betty Neels
NOT FAR ENOUGH Margaret Pargeter
DISHONEST WOMAN Jessica Steele

On sale where you buy paperbacks. If you require further information or have any difficulty obtaining them, write to: Mills & Boon Reader Service, PO Box 236, Thornton Road, Croydon, Surrey CR9 3RU, England.

Mills & Boon
the rose of romance

 **ROMANCE**

Variety is the spice of romance

Each month, Mills & Boon publish new romances. New stories about people falling in love. A world of variety in romance – from the best writers in the romantic world. Choose from these titles in February.

SIGHT OF A STRANGER Sandra Field
A GIRL BEWITCHED Marjorie Lewty
DUELLING FIRE Anne Mather
PLAY OUR SONG AGAIN Lynsey Stevens
DANCE OF THE SNAKE Yvonne Whittal
THE DARK ABYSS Robyn Donald
THE FROZEN JUNGLE Jane Donnelly
NO MAN OF HER OWN Violet Winspear
MEETING AT MIDNIGHT Flora Kidd
HOME TO MORNING STAR Margaret Way

On sale where you buy paperbacks. If you require further information or have any difficulty obtaining them, write to: Mills & Boon Reader Service, PO Box 236, Thornton Road, Croydon, Surrey CR9 3RU, England.

Mills & Boon
the rose of romance

*M*asquerade
Historical Romances

*I*ntrigue
excitement
romance

KING'S PURITAN
by Jean Evans
To Verity Ashbourne, a secret follower of the King, the advent
of Richard Kingston, the commander of a troop of Roundheads
billeted at her home is a threat to the hopes of all royalists.
She despises all he stands for, so why does her heart play
the traitor?

THAT SWEET ENEMY
by Marjorie May
Mary Burns is travelling through Europe with her friends when
Napoleon orders the arrest of all British subjects on French
territory. The enigmatic Captain Armand Dufour offers safe
passes for the whole party – on condition that Mary remains
behind as his wife. If her situation really is so terrible, why does
she fail to take advantage of the opportunities to escape?

Look out for these titles in your local paperback shop from
12th February 1982

FREE
information leaflet about the Mills & Boon Reader Service

It's very easy to subscribe to the Mills & Boon Reader Service. As a regular reader, you can enjoy a whole range of special benefits. Bargain offers. Big cash savings. Your own free Reader Service newsletter, packed with knitting patterns, recipes, competitions and exclusive book offers.

We send you the very latest titles each month, postage and packing free – no hidden extra charges. There's absolutely no commitment – you receive books for only as long as you want.

We'll gladly send you details. Simply send the coupon – or drop us a line for details about the Mills & Boon Reader Service Subscription Scheme.

Post to: Mills & Boon Reader Service, P.O. Box 236, Thornton Road, Croydon, Surrey CR9 3RU, England.
*Please note – READERS IN SOUTH AFRICA please write to: Mills & Boon Reader Service of Southern Africa, Private Bag X3010, Randburg 2125, S. Africa.

Mills & Boon

FREE
Mills & Boon Reader Service Catalogue

The Mills & Boon Reader Service Catalogue lists all the romances that are currently in stock. So if there are any titles that you cannot obtain or have missed in the past, you can get the romances you want DELIVERED DIRECT to your home.

The Reader Service Catalogue is free. Send for it today and we'll send you your copy by return of post.

☐ Please send me details of the Mills & Boon Subscription Scheme.

☐ Please send me my free copy of the Reader Service Catalogue.

BLOCK LETTERS, PLEASE

NAME (Mrs/Miss) _____ EP2

ADDRESS _____

_____

COUNTY/COUNTRY _____ POST/ZIP CODE _____

the rose of romance

Three great Doctor Nurse Romances to look out for this month

There are now three Doctor Nurse Romances for you
to look out for and enjoy every month.
These are the titles for February.

THE NEW PUPIL MIDWIFE
by Lisa Cooper

From the moment pupil-midwife Sally Ashford encounters
Matthew Tregonna, senior registrar at the Princess Beatrice
Hospital, sparks fly. So how could she possibly fall in love with
Matthew when she doesn't even like him?

STAFF NURSE AT ST HELEN'S
by Clare Lavenham

When Nurse Melanie Lister leaves home to share a flat she is
disturbed to find that Andrew Forbes, a new house surgeon, is to be
one of her flatmates. She is determined to dislike him, so why is she
so concerned when he falls gravely ill?

APPLE ISLAND
by Gladys Fullbrook

Paula's success in her final nursing exam coincides with her fiancé
abruptly breaking off their engagement. To recover from the blow,
she joins the Tasmanian Tourist Nursing Service – and finds a
new life, and a new love.

On sale where you buy Mills & Boon romances

The Mills & Boon rose is the rose of romance